THE PERFECT LANDSCAPE

THE PERFECT LANDSCAPE

RAGNA SIGURDARDOTTIR

TRANSLATED BY SARAH BOWEN

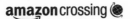

Text copyright © 2009 by Ragna Sigurdardottir
English translation copyright © 2012 by Sarah Bowen

Printed in the United States of America.

The Perfect Landscape was first published in 2009 by Forlagid as *Hið Fullkomna landslag*. Translated from Icelandic by Sarah Bowen. Published in English by AmazonCrossing in 2012.

Published by AmazonCrossing
P.O. Box 400818
Las Vegas, NV 89140

ISBN-13: 9781612184319
ISBN-10: 1612184316
Library of Congress Control Number: 2012911053

1

A LANDSCAPE WITH BIRCH TREES

Hanna steps onto the street. Inhaling the cold, damp, dismal darkness makes her gasp for breath. The dark air smells of rain, wet tarmac, and car exhaust with a hint of saltwater and seaweed. Even when she closes her eyes there's no doubt she's back home. Tucking her head down, she wraps her scarf tightly around her neck, pulls her woolly hat down to her eyes, and walks toward the town center. She hurries along, looking down at the sidewalk, ignoring the street scene around her, which is so very familiar. Seeing a pinkish light from a fast-food outlet reflected in the puddles on the wet asphalt, she peers through the rain and the ugliness of the square takes her by surprise— she had forgotten how bleak downtown Reykjavik can be.

She heads for the Annexe, the city's art gallery. In her head Hanna is still in Holland, where it's cold but calm, like in the painting she's fond of—*Winter Landscape with Skaters and Bird Trap*. It depicts a still and frosty day, roofs laden with snow, skaters all muffled up on a frozen canal, and a bird trap on the bank. For a moment the painting is vividly before her, and then she sees Heba's face, pale in the faint morning light at the railway station in Amsterdam, an auburn curl trailing down the dark blue woolen coat she got for Christmas. Hanna raises an imaginary foil to keep at bay how much she is missing her daughter and walks briskly across the pavement in front of the gallery, where the gusts of wind are sharpest. She tries not to think about Frederico, her Italian husband and father of Heba. They have been married for nearly twenty years, and now their relationship is going through a rough patch.

The Annexe extends from the main building out onto the square; the architect didn't have displaying works of art in mind when he designed this exhibition space for contemporary art. Transparency and flow may currently be all the rage, but it's hardly prudent to put up a glass building in a city that witnesses weekend binge drinking. One pane sports the illegible orange initials of its graffitist; another is covered by a piece of plywood, probably broken over the weekend. Monday morning, Hanna muses. Should the Annexe's funds really be spent on such repairs? Half running the last few feet to the entrance, she attempts to decipher the scribble on the glass without success.

———

Baldur is standing by the window in the meeting room on the second floor, looking out. The gallery's acquisitions committee is meeting, and everyone is present apart from Hanna and Kristin. He glances across at Thor, the lawyer, and, detecting his impatience, looks back to see Hanna running across. Baldur rushes out into the corridor, down the stairs toward the entrance, his keys jangling in his pocket. When he gets to the lobby he presses a button on the reception desk and the door opens. Hanna walks in and greets him—they know each other from their art college days. They look at one another for a moment, and Baldur unconsciously runs his hand through his thick red hair, which is just beginning to fade; the backs of his hands are more freckled than they used to be too.

"I saw you from the window," he says. "Recognized your gait immediately."

Hanna's eyes crinkle when she smiles. When she laughs they almost disappear, but nothing else about her gives the impression of an Asian origin. Her smooth brown hair is totally European, her face is only memorable when she smiles or laughs, and her movements are unremarkable except when she's fencing on the piste.

"It's good to meet an old acquaintance on your first day in a new job," she says, taking off her soaking wet hat and flicking raindrops off her coat as they walk up the stairs, her leather boots resounding on the tiled steps.

"We're just about to begin. Kristin, the director of the gallery, is on the way," explains Baldur as he shows Hanna into the meeting room. Hanna smiles nervously at the three faces turned to greet her. She hasn't been in a management position before and doesn't know which of the three will be working for her, but the job description mentioned two staff.

Baldur introduces her. "This is Agusta, assistant head of exhibitions. She was quite the asset to Bjorn, your predecessor." Agusta nods at Hanna. "Steinn is in charge of conservation and looks after the premises," adds Baldur.

Steinn's age is hard to gauge; he could be five years older or younger than Hanna. He stands up and greets her with a firm handshake; his hand is big and bony. His eyes remind Hanna of blue-gray basalt, smooth, hard, but genial as if warmed by the sun. Hanna is still holding his hand when he quickly drops his eyes and lets go, as if she were being too intimate.

Baldur continues the introductions. "This is Thor, our legal expert," he says. "He has special knowledge of copyright law." Thor rises halfway out of his seat and greets Hanna politely. He is short with graying hair and steel-rimmed spectacles and that rounded face that comes from too many three-course meals in good restaurants, but muscular nonetheless. A lawyer who frequents the gym, thinks Hanna, who has herself practiced fencing for many years, which is enough physical exercise for her.

Taking a seat opposite Steinn and Agusta, Hanna notices an oil painting standing on an easel at the end of the table. It's a landscape painting remarkably like the work of Gudrun Johannsdottir, one of the country's foremost twentieth-century painters. The painting could well be from the series that Hanna knows well, painted before the war, before Gudrun went to Paris, where she carried on her studies, having finished at the Royal Academy in Copenhagen.

The painting is small—a grove of birch trees in the foreground, a mountain on the right, which looks like Mount Baula, and a whitish-blue sky in the distance. The style is realist but has romantic undertones, and there is a hint of Cezanne in the way the canvas is divided up. The brushstrokes have that firm rhythm that Hanna is so familiar with from Gudrun's work.

She leans back in her chair to take in the picture and catches Steinn's eye. He gives her an almost imperceptible grin and she responds with a glimmer of a smile before looking away. She's not going to start her new role exchanging looks when she doesn't know their significance.

There is an aura of politeness around the meeting table; no one refers to the painting.

Puffing and panting, Kristin eventually arrives and shakes Hanna's hand. She exudes a love of her work and total commitment; her dark, speckled-gray eyes look straight into Hanna's as she welcomes her to the group. Kristin has an agitated manner, but that's misleading because when she talks she's clear and concise and comes straight to the point. She sits down at the head of the table next to the painting and launches in.

"How do you like it?" she asks. No one responds; they haven't been told anything about the painting or the meeting's real agenda.

"Elisabet Valsdottir has given us this work of art," Kristin continues proudly. "As you can see, it's clearly by Gudrun Johannsdottir. Elisabet bought it at auction in Copenhagen recently for eight million kronur."

Hanna remembers reading that Gudrun held exhibitions of her work in Copenhagen sometime before the war. Those paintings have not all found their way home to Iceland; some of the sales were not recorded and other works have yet to be uncovered. This one turned up by chance, through some secondhand dealer or from up in an attic somewhere, and then came up for auction. This is one of Gudrun's most appealing pictures, she muses, contemplating the birches, the interplay of colors, their twisted trunks and vibrant foliage. The painting displays a regularity, indicating the direction Gudrun would later take; she has given the twisted birches, which are really no more than shrubs, the true air of a forest tree.

"Elisabet Valsdottir?" asks Hanna.

Kristin gives her a look of surprise. "Don't you know who she is?" she asks brusquely, to which Hanna shakes her head. New faces have become prominent in society since she's been away, and she hasn't kept up-to-date. "She owns a chain of coffee shops that have sprung up all over the place. Elisabet has a keen interest in art and runs her own gallery. She's married to one of the richest men in the country," she adds and mentions a name Hanna has seen in the papers.

"This painting came to light when the estate of a Danish butcher and wealthy storekeeper, Christian Holst, was put up for auction after his widow died last year. The couple owned a large collection of paintings. He bought the majority from the well-known Danish collector, Elisabeth Hansen. She collected abstract works, most of which she bought from artists who later became part of the CoBrA avant-garde movement. But the old guy was partial to landscapes. There was a lyrical side to him. I met him once. He knew his art and may well have bought this painting by Gudrun himself," Kristin explains.

Kristin takes off her glasses to wipe them. "Of course, we'll need to examine the painting before we exhibit it," she says. "I don't want the papers getting wind of it before we've done that. We'll do this as we normally would. This is a real bonus for us. Of course, as you know, our funds don't stretch to a work of art like this one." She smiles, and under the surface Hanna senses her determination and single-mindedness. This is a woman not to be argued with.

"Well then, what d'you say?" Kristin asks without waiting for an answer. Glancing occasionally at the painting, Baldur and Thor talk in undertones. Kristin is chatting about coffee with a short woman who just tapped on the door and strode straight in.

"Edda dear," she says. "This is Hanna. She's taking over the Annexe from Bjorn. She's just come across from Amsterdam. You just arrived yesterday, didn't you, Hanna?" Hanna nods in response and says hello to Edda.

"Edda fixes everything around here," says Kristin, laughing. "She's worked here at the gallery since it started. She's a real treasure. I don't suppose there are any Danish pastries today, are there?" Kristin asks, and Edda is already on it; on her way out she smiles at Hanna, who immediately takes to her.

Hanna contemplates the painting. Whose responsibility will it be to examine it? What is the gallery's organization; how is it structured? As conservator, it must be Steinn's job to see to this sort of thing. From this one brief meeting she has the impression that the gallery is a small closed world and the staff function like a family. They have all worked here for a long time—Edda from the outset, Baldur for at least ten years. Steinn looks very much at home here, and Hanna knows that Kristin has been the director for about five years. Even the young woman, Agusta, seems to be one of the family.

Kristin interrupts her thoughts. "Hanna, you and Steinn look into this. Bjorn was damn good at writing reports. I hope you're going to follow in his footsteps," she says.

"Hanna wrote her dissertation on Gudrun," Baldur interjects, as if coming to her defense. Hanna looks at him in surprise; she doesn't need someone to defend her and doesn't appreciate being put in that position unbidden. As director of the Annexe, she is also surprised to be asked to take this task on. Her area of expertise is managing exhibitions and the history of landscape painting. But it is true, she did write a dissertation on Gudrun and knows her work well. In her mind she slips into the en garde position, ready for anything.

"Yes, that's right, I did. In fact, with particular reference to this period of Gudrun's career," she says calmly, imagining herself pressing the tip of her foil against Baldur's chest, pinning him to the wall while she talks. She is here on her own merits; this is her job and she doesn't need anyone meddling.

Baldur doesn't say anything further; it's the lawyer, Thor, who cuts in. "Didn't Gudrun hold an auction of her paintings in Copenhagen before the war?" he asks, looking to Hanna for confirmation.

"Indeed she did," Hanna replies. "And in all likelihood this was painted either in her student days or the summer before she left for Paris. It looks like one of her woodscapes. It's possible that Gudrun sold it at an exhibition held in the Larsen Gallery on Hojbroplads, or maybe at the auction you mentioned—which she held to fund further training in Paris."

After a moment's silence Hanna adds, "It looks to me like this painting is a really valuable acquisition." She looks at the painting and particularly at the mountain in the background. It can only be Mount Baula, actually painted as a straightforward triangle and typical of Gudrun's style. This is undoubtedly a boost for the gallery. The Annexe and the gallery are clearly not such separate entities as Hanna had thought; the gallery is simply too small for that. Everyone has to pull together here, and Hanna's role needn't necessarily be limited to the Annexe. That may not be a bad thing. Straightaway on her first day she's been given a very responsible project, which shows that she is trusted and that her knowledge in a particular field is known within the gallery.

Hanna gets up from the table to look at the picture more carefully. Kristin joins her, and they discuss the aesthetics of the painting; they talk about Gudrun's career and her other works the gallery owns. Kristin is easy to talk to, but Hanna senses that she would stand her ground. She is clearly the sort of woman who gets her way. Her dappled neck scarf may be like a matador's muleta, but Kristin lets the bull charge where it will—she has her own strategy in play. Hanna will be on her guard.

Behind her she can hear Baldur and Thor talking about a new golf course on the outskirts of the city and the door closing. When she looks around, Steinn has left. Edda returns shortly after with a tray, and the meeting dissolves into drinking coffee and eating Danish pastries. Kristin does most of the talking, telling the others about a dinner she was invited to in Copenhagen not long ago with the former Icelandic president. Aha, thinks Hanna. Snob. Maybe the neck scarf is a sign of vanity, a desire for glitz—a chasing after the wind. But perhaps being a snob is in some ways a positive attribute for the director of an art gallery. If you must give up some of your time to various social duties, such as openings, you might as well enjoy it. Kristin doesn't refer to Elisabet Valsdottir again, but Hanna would like to learn more.

"Has Elisabet donated to the gallery in the past?" she asks cautiously and is careful not to indicate that she thinks anything out of the ordinary about the gift.

"Elisabet and I are old friends," Kristin replies, "but she hasn't given the gallery anything until now. This was just so ideal and she told me she couldn't help but think of me when she saw this at the auction." Kristin positively glows as she divulges this information, and Hanna is careful to smile in response, but she is surprised. In Holland a gallery director would have kept such details to herself, made light of her connection to the donor.

In and of itself there's nothing significant about the gallery accepting such a superb gift. Why should Kristin refuse a present from a good friend who also happens to be one of the richest women in the country? But it does make Hanna wonder what Elisabet might take upon herself to give the gallery next and how they would react if the gift wasn't up to the gallery's standards. Kristin would surely refuse such a gift, wouldn't she? And if it became a habit among wealthy businessmen to give the gallery gifts in order to bathe their reputation in the art world's limelight, then wouldn't the gallery's artworks become a motley collection? Hanna looks back at the picture. It speaks for itself, and she stops worrying and quietly admires the painting.

The meeting is over. Before she leaves, Kristin reminds them of the staff meeting later in the week. "We need to go over the program," she says, "so we're all singing from the same song sheet."

Hanna sits quietly for a moment, looking at the painting while the others leave. Baldur is on the phone, talking in hushed tones. She wishes Steinn had not slipped out so soon. Something about his calm manner intrigues her. His job is not clear. Is he really conservator and caretaker combined? Perhaps that's feasible in such a small gallery.

Exhaustion washes over her, a combination of jet lag and lack of sleep. To summon the energy to get up and tackle all that lies ahead, a new job and new colleagues, she gazes at the scene in the painting—drawing strength from the vitality in the colors of the foliage, the uncompromising mountain, and the white light of the sky.

Gudrun didn't paint many woodscapes during her career; for obvious reasons this has never been a common motif for Icelandic artists. They have tended to focus on mountains. And Icelandic landscape painting didn't come into being until late in the nineteenth century. Up until that point the landscape had been perceived as nothing but rugged pathways and rough trackless terrain. Hanna observes the colors on the ground and the light on the tree trunks. It's as if Gudrun has bent nature to her own will, given it a balance that it doesn't possess, a tranquility that is not real, an immutability that Hanna knows nature does not have but that she longs to find, and she forgets herself for a moment.

When Steinn comes in with a roll of polyethylene, Hanna hurriedly gets to her feet because she wants to have a chat. But neither his manner nor the way he sets about the task invites interaction or interruption. He silently rolls the polyethylene out on the floor; takes the painting down from the easel; cuts the plastic with a penknife; and, wrapping the painting up very carefully, goes out with the knife and the roll of polyethylene under one arm and the painting under the other.

Hanna senses Baldur looking over to her as he finishes his phone call. He looks like he is hoping she will wait for him; maybe he wants to show her around the premises and the offices himself. What Hanna wants is to slip out into the corridor and follow Steinn, but that would look odd so she turns and waits for Baldur instead. He puts the phone in his pocket and smiles at her.

"You haven't changed a bit," he says in a friendly tone when it's just the two of them. Hanna isn't prepared for this. He talks as if they know each other better than she remembers, or like a supervisor to his junior. Maybe it's just the Icelandic way. Has she forgotten how people talk over here? She doesn't respond, and he carries on. "So you're just taking over. You've done extremely well for yourself."

As if he hadn't really expected her to. But perhaps he's only trying to be friendly. Hanna isn't sure, and despite their old acquaintance she finds herself on her guard with him as she was with Kristin.

They go out into the corridor and walk down the stairs. Baldur gives Hanna a general outline of his role at the gallery. He is head of exhibitions, deals more with actually executing projects than generating ideas. He is responsible for producing the gallery's publications and has been from the outset, from way before the Annexe came into being. It's evidently very important to maintain good relations with Baldur, even though Hanna hasn't quite worked out which reins of power he really holds. A little gallery in a small country, she thinks. Maybe the responsibilities of the employees are not as delineated as Hanna is accustomed to, the rules aren't as inflexible, and perhaps everything happens more smoothly here than she has experienced before, but that doesn't necessarily simplify matters.

While they're walking around the premises, Hanna recalls what she knows about Baldur's career after they graduated. Things went tolerably well for him; he even exhibited in the National Gallery, was a bit of a star for a while. He also had a contract with another gallery to exhibit his work, but that ended long ago. Hanna can't remember reading about any exhibition of his work in recent years. Baldur's zenith was around the time of neo-Expressionism; the style suited him well. She can picture the exhibitions becoming fewer and farther between as the years went by, how he didn't succeed in forging relations abroad and had sated the limited market at home. In the end a regular monthly salary and a less demanding relationship with art than that involved in creating from scratch had given him more satisfaction in life than relentlessly carrying on painting pictures in a style that had gone out of fashion. Baldur was only one of many she knew who had taken this path.

Now drawings, craftwork, and the personal approach are back in vogue and painting is in a state of flux, Hanna muses. Surely Baldur wouldn't consider going back to painting, would he? Can an artist who has put his art on the back burner for years on end get the chance to come back?

At least Baldur was once up with the times. As a young-ster Hanna had only had eyes for landscapes, which weren't in fashion even then. In their different ways Hanna's parents had each encouraged her to go on and study art. Most of the people back home thought she would become a painter because she drew so well. It wasn't until she got to art college that she real-ized there was more to art than being a draftsman. Gradually she had also realized that she was more interested in reading, looking, and interpreting. She didn't have that edge that was needed to paint convincing landscapes when they were no lon-ger the in thing. She painted the same motifs over and over but was always dissatisfied, couldn't quite achieve what she was aiming for, and didn't even really know what that was. History of art lectures were her favorite, when she sat in the semidark-ness and watched the color slides being projected onto the screen—even then it was the landscape paintings that moved her. Portrait paintings with landscapes in the background or fifteenth- and sixteenth-century paintings depicting landscapes through a window; the confined world of peasants in the paintings of Brueghel the Elder and the Younger in the sixteenth and seventeenth centuries; the expansive cloudscapes of the Dutch Golden Age; the emotional response to nature in Romanticism of the nineteenth century, when man stood alone in the face of forces greater than himself; the glorious use of color in Impressionism.

Following her course at art college, Hanna went on to study art at the university and then to Amsterdam to complete her master's, where she concentrated on the history of landscape paintings in Europe in the seventeenth century. Curating came later, somewhat unexpectedly, just as fencing had. Heba had wanted to learn fencing, but in the end it was Hanna who became hooked on it.

Hanna and Baldur don't stop on their tour around the gallery, nor do they talk about the current exhibit on display until Hanna pauses at a painting on the second-floor landing.

"Ah yes," she says. "*Composition in Blue*, isn't it? By Sigfus? I've only ever seen a photo of it."

"There was a great hullabaloo about it," Baldur comments. "But the painting's not bad."

"It's smaller than I thought," says Hanna. "And the blue color isn't as piercing as I remember." They stand there for a moment, looking at an abstract painting by Sigfus Gunnarsson, one of the nation's most celebrated artists, which had been exciting news when it was donated to the gallery the year before.

Baldur shows Hanna all the nooks and crannies. The gallery's artworks are stored in cellars and storage rooms all over the city, and their exhibition spaces are designed so displays can easily be changed. Once or twice a year the gallery focuses on the history of Icelandic painting, putting on exhibitions from their own collection, but otherwise the story of the nation's art isn't available to the general public. Their collection is limited, as are their funds for investing in works of art. If they buy the work of younger artists, then there will be gaps in the collection of older works; if they try to plug the missing gaps of history, then a whole generation of contemporary artists will be lost to the gallery.

Baldur seems very much at home here and has the power to open and close doors. Hanna wonders how well he and Kristin get along. Sometimes men find it difficult to have a female boss. And won't she herself be his boss to some extent? The Annexe is an avant-garde exhibition space, the gallery's trump card in international terms, and in recent years it has exhibited famous foreign artists alongside Icelandic ones. Now she is the new director. Her position is undoubtedly more important than his; despite everything, he is her subordinate.

Eventually Baldur opens a door at ground level leading to a large office with enormous windows along the full length of one wall. In the middle of the room is a large partitioned workstation, where Hanna spots Agusta and Edda at their computers. Under the window wall is a long table covered in papers, cans, and containers, with a computer at the far end. This office space has a modern feel to it—as with the Annexe, the idea is that natural daylight should flood unhindered into the room; even the concrete floor has a trendy clear varnish. Outside, dawn hasn't yet broken, and fluorescent bulbs light up the space.

"Kristin and I have offices on the second floor, where the education department and management, marketing, and publicity sections are," says Baldur. "The rest of the staff is here, but Steinn also has a workshop in the basement. This is Bjorn's desk," he adds, stopping at a desk in the middle of the cluster of cubicles and looking at Hanna, who stares at him blankly.

Who is Bjorn? Then it registers. She is taking over from Bjorn and this is her desk. Hanna assumed she would have her own office and two assistants. That was how the job description read. This is not quite what she'd envisaged, and for a second she feels like a fool. She'd forgotten how Iceland operates on a small scale. Obviously the gallery has no money. The Annexe exists more in theory than in reality when there's no funding. She concentrates on hiding her thoughts. The job doesn't revolve around having your own office. The work doesn't get done by sitting alone within four walls. This can only work out better. In a flash, as if she's back on the fencing piste, she turns the situation to her advantage. In her head she moves into the en garde position, running her fingers lightly along the grip. Then she smiles her most winning smile at Baldur.

"Excellent!" she says. "This is great—I really like it."

Carefully maintaining the gleam in her eyes, Hanna observes Baldur closely. He fiddles nervously with the ring on his finger. That worked, she thinks to herself. He knew this would take me by surprise. He was watching me. But I knocked him off guard.

Hanna smiles at Edda and Agusta, who are sitting on either side of Bjorn's desk, *her* desk. Thoughts flash across her mind. Baldur's role is not what she had thought. Now an unexpected divide has formed between them. A whole floor, in fact. She thought she was taking on a more responsible role than his but was probably mistaken, at least if the structure of the office space is anything to go by.

"Maybe you'd rather not sit here? Right in the middle of the chaos?" Baldur asks as if he's read her thoughts. "Of course, it's often hectic here, not exactly peaceful. I could maybe find you a quiet corner if you'd prefer?"

But Hanna has no intention of being stuck in a corner somewhere. In her head she holds her position on the piste, her foil raised and maintaining priority of attack. She doesn't shift her gaze from the desk and replies without hesitation, "No, this is absolutely ideal. I much prefer to be at the hub. That's how I've always envisaged the Annexe. I like to be around people, where it's all happening." Hanna smiles inwardly because nothing could be further from the truth when it comes to her work style. She has always needed peace and quiet, and she struggles with the hustle and bustle of people coming and going around her. Now she is being put to the test and she is in battle mode.

Hanna looks over at Agusta, who flashes her a quick smile as she clicks on her e-mails and answers the phone. She is young. Maybe twenty-five, Hanna guesses. The roots of her dyed blonde hair show through her asymmetrical bob, and she's wearing dark eye makeup. She looks as if she makes an effort to dress fashionably. Hanna recognizes the dress label and the brand of shoe; her clothes are a tasteful mix of secondhand and new, of the flea market and designer labels. Agusta is evidently at pains to show how capable and how busy she is in her job. Hanna recognizes the type. This is the diligent student. The girl who is so bright and together. Very alert, always willing and able, finishes all her assignments before the deadline and is not afraid to tell someone else that something could be done better.

Recognizing a little of herself in Agusta, both in the conscientious student and her underlying ambition, Hanna tries to contain her irrational hostility. It's unlikely Agusta knows that Hanna has an ally in Baldur, an old acquaintance who might come in handy. And Agusta is young. I know better, Hanna thinks to herself. Ought to know better. She simply smiles politely to Agusta while Baldur carries on talking. Hanna realizes that he likes the sound of his own voice and it's best to let him go on.

"Agusta has taken on the task of keeping track of the reports about the state of artworks in public places," he says, patting a pile of reports on her desk. "It had become a pressing task, so it's good that you're here to oversee it. This has been on the back burner since Bjorn left, and the Annexe deals with this, as you know."

Hanna doesn't reply immediately. Silence is going to be her main weapon on her first day. Best not to let anything get to you and to show no reaction. Yes, she's truly back home again—dealing with what's thrown at you is all part of the game. Having charge of outdoor artworks owned by the city is obviously a large part of the job. In all probability the largest part, so it's not surprising that no one mentioned it when she was asked to come on board. She can see plainly that this aspect of the work will be time-consuming, complex, and a drain on resources. How many artworks in public spaces does the city own? And what sort of a state are they likely to be in, given the broken pane and graffiti she saw on the Annexe on her way in? Maybe it's no wonder that her predecessor, Bjorn, escaped to Denmark.

"Yes, of course I'm aware of this," says Hanna. She gives it no further thought for the moment because Baldur is introducing her to her colleagues on the other side of the partition.

"This is Margret, she deals with the accounts. Vala looks after the archives and registry, and over there is Steinn's desk," he says, pointing to a long table under the window. Hanna shakes hands with the two women and is relieved when Baldur finally goes to get on with his own work.

Sitting down at Bjorn's desk, now hers, she sighs with relief and opens her briefcase—a large, soft leather case of indeterminate color that has been her companion for years and was a present from Frederico, her Italian husband of nearly twenty years. In it is a box of assorted chocolates that she's brought from Amsterdam to offer around on her first day in her new job. The lid has a picture from one of the most famous illuminated manuscripts in the history of Europe from the Middle Ages, *Les Tres Riches Heures du Duc de Berry*. In the Middle Ages it was the custom to have a book of hours, handwritten with prayers for each hour of the day and a calendar showing the hours of the day and the months of the year. The month of January adorns the chocolate box and shows the Duke of Berry dressed in rich blue robes patterned like a peacock's tail. He is sitting at a table piled high with food, surrounded by his courtiers and precious possessions.

Holding the box in her hands, Hanna hesitates for a moment, then opens it and hands it to Edda. It's difficult to determine how old Edda is; she's cheerful but looks careworn, and her voice is slightly gruff. Maybe she's a smoker or drinks too much. Or maybe it's just weariness? Icelandic winters, lots of children, low salary, and high inflation? For a second Hanna becomes aware of her own appearance, smooth brown hair brushed neatly in a ponytail, a high-quality designer sweater in unassuming lilac-gray tones, a well-tailored skirt, and Italian leather boots. She's had a good life.

"We must have some coffee with this," says Edda instead of taking a chocolate from the box. Shortly after, all six of them, Hanna, Agusta, Edda, Vala, Margret, and Steinn, who has just come back in, are sitting in the corner drinking coffee.

"This is the Duke of Berry," explains Hanna, taking off the lid and handing the box around. "He was a powerful, wealthy man at the turn of the fifteenth century. And an art connoisseur. He employed the Limbourg brothers to illuminate a book of hours and an almanac. This is January, the month for giving New Year's gifts. A long time ago in Europe, New Year's gifts were really just like Christmas presents."

Steinn gently runs his finger over the shiny paper on the lid as if to get the feel of its quality. His touch is light. Hanna momentarily watches his fingertips gliding over the surface of the picture, over the duke's blue robe, before looking away as though she'd witnessed something she shouldn't have. "The duke had seventeen castles and stately homes in France," she says.

"Look, there are some animals on the table as well," Agusta points out. "I know these pictures. We talked about them in art history, but I've never examined them in such detail."

"He also collected exotic animals," replies Hanna. "Peacocks, camels, and dromedaries, to name but a few. The dogs you see on the table are a special breed of dog that can be traced back to the Arctic hounds used for pulling sleds. I once wrote an essay on this illuminated manuscript," she adds as if defending her specialist knowledge about the breed of dog depicted on the banquet table of a five-hundred-year-old picture. "Animals were part of his collection, and they had special keepers to look after them. He owned jewels as well and had a large collection of rubies. And books, illuminated vellum manuscripts in expensive colors, like lapis lazuli imported from the East."

Steinn looks at her a moment, like he knows what she is talking about. "The rich and powerful of today cannot display such treasures," he says, and his voice is reminiscent of his eyes, firm and resolute.

"And when he died there wasn't any money to pay for the funeral," Hanna says in response. "He'd spent it all on costly items."

"He was dead anyway by then," says Steinn. "You can't take your money with you." He gives a wry smile, as if the thought that we're all equal on our deathbeds pleases him.

"He's a communist and antimaterialist," says Agusta by way of explanation or maybe to tease Steinn, but he doesn't rise to it or even deign to look her way.

"Kids might just do something other than deface walls if this society had some gumption," he says, gazing out of the window as if he were alone. Hanna knows she will get on well with him. He doesn't seem the sort to make a mountain out of a molehill. "Well, I've got plenty to do," says Steinn a moment later, and they all get up from the table. Sitting back down at Bjorn's desk, Hanna looks through some papers and turns on the computer.

Agusta suddenly glances over at Hanna. "I'm printing this out for you," she says and then starts talking. And can she talk, more than Baldur. She has a gently chirping voice with a pushy undertone; she talks without pausing, the words just streaming out of her effortlessly and yet concisely.

She's a pro, Hanna thinks, trying to contain her tiredness. It takes all her energy to follow Agusta without losing the thread. Agusta's youthfulness and the way she blinks remind Hanna of Heba. Agusta is telling Hanna about her work with Bjorn, Hanna's predecessor. She talks about a small international group of independent curators who she works with. She tells her how she and Bjorn liked to work, and finally Hanna understands why Agusta appears unenthusiastic about having a new boss. Bjorn's approach had evidently been very hands-off and he'd let Agusta have free rein, but now those days are over.

"I envision this as a joint project," Hanna says when Agusta asks her about her plans, at the same time apologizing for asking Hanna at the wrong moment. She says she realizes Hanna obviously needs to familiarize herself with the details. But she still asks. She can't help herself. Hanna tries to say as little as possible. She mentions the idea of landscape paintings and art in public spaces, a combined exhibition in the spring. Agusta is interested. It probably wouldn't matter what she said; Agusta would find any idea interesting. You could easily extend this concept, run with it in any number of ways. The joy of making something happen is so tangible, something you believe in so passionately that the desire to make a difference is so strong. Agusta is just beginning. Hanna has stopped listening and is watching her speak, watching her nostrils flare, and it occurs to Hanna that Agusta will undoubtedly go far and could be pushy if she needed to be. In her mind's eye she sees a column of steam rising from her nose like on the folkloristic painting

by Jon Stefansson in which the ghost bull, Thorgeirsboli, domi-
nates the center of the scene. Unwittingly she gives a smile, and
Agusta looks at her, perplexed.

"Yes, absolutely," says Hanna without having a clue what
Agusta has just been talking about. She promptly feels bad
because Agusta is probably lovely—she doesn't appear quick to
take offense, and even though she babbles on, she knows when
to shut up because she quickly finishes her monologue and
leaves to make a call, scribbling as she speaks. Hanna is about
to turn back to her computer when Steinn appears with a pile
of papers. He clears his throat, and Hanna waits to hear what's
on his mind.

"I, er, I've got some more reports on the state of the outdoor artworks," he says. "We'll have to make a start repairing
many of them in the spring. And then there's a lot of vandalism. That's on the increase. Since the city banned graffiti about
a year ago it's gone crazy, and we can't keep up with it. These
youngsters have no respect for art. Agusta has started to log
some of the reports, and here's the rest. It would be good if you
could have a look at these as soon as possible," he says. "I'm
going to have a look at a vandalized sculpture in the woods by
Oskjuhlid, which we heard about this morning," he says, referring to the hill on the southern outskirts of the city. "Do you
think you could come with me? Then you'll have a better idea
of what's going on."

"Delighted to," Hanna agrees without a moment's hesitation. She'd enjoy going out in the car with Steinn. Then she
glances at the reports. The title page reads, "A Report on the
Condition of Artworks Owned by the City." There is a photo of
a sculpture covered in graffiti with a detailed description and

an assessment of what needs to be done to bring it back to its original condition. Hanna rests her hand on the pile. In the background Agusta's voice chirps in a familiar fashion, and out of the corner of her eye she's aware of Edda briskly coming and going. She looks at Steinn's back as he pores over something on the long table. He has made space for a desk lamp with a strong bulb, which floodlights the table and is reflected in the windowpane above.

She can't see the two women on the other side of the partition, but she can hear the tap-tap of the keyboards, and every so often a phone rings; their voices are low and she can't make out the words. Outside it has finally started to get light, and the familiar outline of Mount Esja is visible, dark against the faint gray morning light.

It's past midday when Steinn comes over to Hanna and asks whether she's up for going across to Oskjuhlid.

On their way out to the parking lot at the back of the gallery, Steinn looks questioningly at Hanna and asks hesitantly, "By the way, would you mind driving?" The question takes her by surprise, but Steinn offers no explanation and she doesn't ask. It's not that he's disagreeable, but he doesn't exactly invite further inquiry. He has a quiet manner, and his responses are measured. Hanna wants to get to know Steinn, and she tries to slow herself down to his rhythm, mentally drawing herself into the preparatory stance. Of course she can drive. What a question! Steinn fishes the car keys out of his pocket and hands them to her. Apart from the file he has tucked under his arm, he reminds her of a farmer on his way out to the cattle shed in his russet-red winter jacket and knitted hat. He has shoved the digital camera, which he'll use to record the damage, into his jacket pocket. His silver-colored ski pole taps on the wet tarmac. Hiking fanatic, thinks Hanna. Definitely goes walking in the mountains on the weekends.

He silently points the ski pole diagonally across the parking lot toward an old blue Volvo. The pay of a conservator or whatever it is he really does at the gallery is clearly nothing to write home about. Hanna wonders whether he has a wife and what she does. She can hardly be in a well-paid job judging by this old banger, which could well belong to a farmer. There aren't any child seats in the back. But if he has children they could be too big for that, she supposes as she gets into the driver's seat, slides it forward, and adjusts the rearview mirror. Steinn keeps quiet in the passenger seat as she pulls out jerkily and stalls the Volvo—she isn't used to manual cars. She wonders if he's on some kind of medication that means he can't drive; yet he drove to work this morning.

Hanna wants to ask him about the sculpture they're going to see and when they should have a look at Gudrun's painting but can't quite bring herself to, so they drive in silence. After a bit Steinn switches on the radio, and for the few minutes it takes to drive from the gallery to the wooded hillside, they listen to announcements and news bulletins. Hanna pricks up her ears when she hears the name of an old friend, Gudny, who is now the minister for justice, mentioned in connection with legislation on young offenders. Then she remembers who Agusta reminds her of—Gudny when she was young. It's the ambitiousness. Underlying, continual, hungry ambition, which will never be fully satisfied. Agusta will go far, she thinks to herself, already on edge. This job may not turn out quite as cushy as she'd imagined back home in Amsterdam.

Gudny's job means she's often in the news, and Hanna has followed her work on Internet news pages. She's looking forward to meeting her, and also Laufey and a few others who were all good friends at secondary school; it's been a long time since the five of them have caught up. She makes up her mind to get in touch with them all as soon as possible. The next news item is about finding funds to build an earthquake museum at Kopasker, a small village in the north of the country. Hanna reaches out and turns the radio off. They've arrived.

They park the car at the bottom of the hill, where the conifers appear dark green in the damp air. At the top, the old water tanks, which used to house the city's hot water supply, now stand empty. On top of them sits an expensive restaurant with a shiny glass roof, whose glistening silver-gray reflects the pewter sky. A footpath of red gravel leads from the parking lot to the edge of the trees. The grass on either side is a yellowy gray after the winter, scattered with puddles. Steinn walks on ahead, his step calm and confident.

When they reach the trees it's like entering another world, timeless and free from the everyday laws of this gloomy January day. The noise of the city dies away. Steinn swings his ski pole; the red of his jacket and the silver stick stand out among the dark conifers. For a second Hanna sees in her mind's eye the painting by Renaissance artist Paolo Uccello, *The Hunt in the Forest*. In this picture men are dressed in red and, either on foot or on horseback, are chasing hares in a dark forest. Some hold white spears, slicing the dark background like the white hunting dogs leaping across the canvas. Uccello's aim in this painting was to demonstrate how convincingly he could portray perspective, which was a novelty at the time. Paolo Uccello can also be translated as Paul the Bird as *uccello* is Italian for *bird*. He was given this nickname because he was fascinated by animals, and especially birds. Steinn is maybe a bit like that, Hanna muses, an eccentric withdrawn from his surroundings. She pictures him sitting at home poring over chemistry books.

On they go in the half-light, barely able to make out anything before them. Under the trees the ground is covered in dry humus and littered with pine needles and cones; the lowest branches have lost their needles. The walk has a hypnotic effect on Hanna, as if she's slipped into a dream and is following the rhythmical tapping of Steinn's stick like a metronome. Then they hear a rustle and she sees something scuttle past in the dusk. Steinn stops suddenly and puts his finger to his lips. For a moment they both stand stock-still, hardly daring to breathe. Out of the gloom two white rabbits stare at them before turning tail, two gray shadows disappearing into the darkness. Unlike the scene in Paul the Bird's painting, it is peaceful here, no hunters shouting and calling, no dogs barking or hooves pounding. Ahead is a hint of daylight, and the path opens out into a clearing.

Here they are met by a memorial to a Norwegian entrepreneur in forestry, his bronze bust crowning a concrete pillar with an inscription on a metal plaque. But the statue is now unrecognizable. Someone has sprayed it with an array of colored paints so that the bronze can no longer be seen. The same is true of the pillar that, quite apart from damage arising from the damp and from moss, has also been liberally spray-painted; the inscription on the plaque is illegible. Broken glass lies scattered all around, as if some people got together with glass bottles for a smash party. There's more broken glass on the statue itself.

They stand there lost for words, taking in this excessive and incomprehensible vandalism, which isn't sloppy and crude but somehow carefully executed. For a moment Steinn covers his eyes with his hand as if in pain.

"We had a call about this this morning," he says slowly. "We don't know when it happened—someone who was out walking here over the weekend tipped us off."

"This is a job for the street-cleaning department," Hanna says for want of something to say. "The broken glass, I mean." She is upset. There's something rather disconcerting about seeing a work of art treated in this way, especially when it's designed to honor someone's memory. It's like a physical assault with no obvious motive.

Steinn walks right up to the pillar and peers at the concrete, running his hand over the rough, soiled surface. Something about his touch catches Hanna's attention, and for a moment they stand in silence while he carefully feels the surface with his fingertips. She feels the slight drizzle on her face, catches the scent of pine needles in the air. She's not on her guard with Steinn; on the contrary, his presence gives her strength. He is a good man, quite simply a good guy.

"I know how we can clean this up," he says slowly but with a smile, as if to reassure her there's no need to worry. "It'll take time, but it's doable. See, the bronze is sealed, the paint won't seep in. And the concrete on the pillar can be sandblasted and cleaned, with nitromors, for example," he says more to himself, lowering his voice.

"The bust can be cleaned with a special preprepared mixture," he adds, loud enough for Hanna to hear. Pulling the camera out of his pocket, he walks around the statue and photographs what needs to be cleaned and repaired. Hanna also circles the work of art, examining the spray-painting for something legible. At one point she can make out some initials, but they are unclear and she can't tell whether or not they are part of the overall graffiti on the statue.

"What do they hope to achieve?" says Hanna more into thin air than looking for an answer.

"It's good to get things fixed," says Steinn, not responding to her question. "Restores your faith in life. Faith that even though things can go badly, it's still possible to get them back on track again."

Hanna looks at him, his trustworthy expression, broad shoulders, and strong hands. She sits down on a bench nearby, in the shadow of the pines. The dark treetops contrast with the leaden sky. The spruces are taller than the pines; some of the tops are bowed or bent over. There are no birds anywhere to be seen. Not a sound can be heard other than Steinn's footsteps as he treads on the gravel around the sculpture. Hanna senses the closeness of the wood. Is it really possible to get your life back on track when something unfortunate happens, as Steinn was saying? She looks at the tree trunks and the dusk. There is something timeless about a wood, no trace of human intervention. The tiredness washes over her again; she stops mulling things over and relaxes.

Five hundred years ago Leonardo da Vinci wrote about the nuances of light in nature, about sunlight dappling on leaves, on the surface of running water. How smoke rising from a bonfire in a forest clearing has a bluish tinge against the dark background. Such as this forest floor. The smoke is bluest if the timber is dry and if the sun's rays reach it, Leonardo wrote, and his words capture a fleeting moment from long ago.

Hanna sits there motionless. Suddenly Steinn is standing before her—he has finished taking the photographs. "All done," he says, and she smiles up at him absentmindedly, because she has managed to forget her troubles for a while. Naturally warmhearted, Steinn smiles back, a smile that lights up his gray eyes. Hanna circles the statue once more, avoiding the broken glass scattered on the ground. They are just about to head back to the gallery when they hear footsteps and a man with a large camera emerges into the clearing. The papers have evidently been informed as well, thinks Hanna as she greets the photographer from the national paper. People don't just phone the gallery; they also call the press. Hanna and Steinn watch as he photographs the damage.

"Have you seen anything this bad before?" asks Hanna, assuming that a newspaper photographer will keep abreast of what's happening.

"I saw a wall downtown the other day that reminds me of this," he replies. "It was similar, a random explosion of paint, not the usual tagging and stuff you get everywhere. This was huge and wild—like this one here."

The vandalism has a paralyzing effect on them, and they fall silent. It's beginning to rain again. Steinn makes a move and turns to Hanna.

"Shall we go?"

They say good-bye to the photographer and don't look back as the camera starts clicking again; maybe the rain will lend the pictures an extra dramatic dimension. Steinn thrusts the folder under his jacket and leads the way back. On reaching the car, Hanna gets in the driver's side without asking.

2

IMAGES OF A PAINTING

One day in late January, Steinn quietly asks Hanna whether she would like to have a look at the painting with him. Just like that, as if it were perfectly normal that he hadn't mentioned it earlier, quite natural that nearly three weeks had gone by since they first saw it, on the day Hanna first started at the gallery. She hadn't mentioned it either; she'd realized straightaway that Steinn was not someone to be hassled. When a gallery is given a work like this, it goes without saying that it's thoroughly scrutinized.

Hanna's role first and foremost is to examine the painting from the point of view of the art historian. To evaluate the work objectively and decide where it fits chronologically in Gudrun's career. To compare it with her other works, look for points of connection with paintings carried out at roughly the same time. To analyze its structure, use of color, and brushstrokes to determine whether these are all characteristic of the artist's style.

Steinn's focus is on the physical aspect of the painting; he looks at it from a technical perspective. Does it need cleaning?

Does it need a new frame? Is there any damage that needs fixing? Has the ownership history been confirmed?

At the agreed time Hanna goes down the steps to the basement, which houses the gallery's storage rooms and where conservation is carried out. She knocks on the door cautiously, which Steinn opens sharply, causing Hanna to shrink back before entering.

This is Steinn's kingdom. A large, bright, well-lit work surface stands in the center; paintings and smaller pictures fill every nook and cranny, standing propped on the floor or leaning up against shelves and cupboards. There is row after row of paintings, drawings, and watercolors. Hanna takes Gudrun's painting from an easel against a wall—*The Birches*, as they call it. The green color is rich in tone under the even, fluorescent light; the whitish-blue of the sky is sparkling; and the outline of Mount Baula is clearly defined as it rises up like a triangle from the birch tops. She stands still, looking at the painting, at the green light dappling on the birch leaves. The height of summer—it was hot when this picture was sketched, perhaps it was painted in situ.

"I'd like to start by looking at Gudrun's sketchbooks from this period, her drawings and watercolors and so on," Hanna says to break the silence. "It would be good to find a sketch of this motif to go with the painting."

Steinn struggles to pull something out of the small plastic bag in his hands. "Well..." he says, pointing her to some shelves farther into the workspace, where Hanna finds boxes marked "Gudrun" filled with sketchbooks and loose drawings. "We can look at those," he finishes as Hanna lays the boxes on the table. "But it'll take time."

Hanna doesn't respond. She doesn't understand what he's driving at, why this would be a waste of time. Hanna responds professionally, in a measured manner. "I'll look through these," she says. "I'll show you if I find something relevant, but we probably don't both need to pore over them."

Steinn finally manages to separate a pair of white cotton gloves from the others in the bag and hands them to Hanna, who slips them on. Steinn is not his usual self, she thinks. He seems nervous, as if he finds this difficult.

They stand over the well-lit table in the center of the room; Hanna lifts a brown folder out of the box and lays it in front of her. Steinn makes no attempt to look at it with her but still stands close by. Seeing the determined set of his mouth, Hanna suddenly becomes very aware of the warmth from his body. Her reaction to this unexpected physical proximity takes her by surprise. Somewhat agitated, she opens the folder.

Flicking carefully through the sketchbooks, she examines the drawings, looking for the angle from which this painting was done, the gnarled birch trees in the foreground and the triangular shaped mountain to the right of the canvas. There are lots of drawings in the folder and even more in the box. She shudders at the thought of going through them all on her own and is surprised at Steinn's sudden lack of cooperation. From her very first day, he has gone out of his way to support her in every way, so much so that it is beginning to grate. She has also noticed how clever he is at subtly exerting his influence in situations with his little silences, facial expressions, and gestures. She has started to look out for these now, and he seldom lets her down; she follows his facial expressions like she was reading her opponent's body movements on the fencing piste.

Now she sees his lower lip stubbornly jutting out and his chin stiffening slightly. Evidently she'll be looking at these sketches on her own. Hanna smiles to herself, almost sure that he's doing the same with her, that he's reading her as much as she is him. He must sense the unspoken friendship that has grown between them from that first day. They have a lot in common; they understand each other even though they don't know one another outside of work. They share a similar sense of humor; their attitude to life is much the same. They are both inclined to keep silent when the situation demands, and a glance is often enough to know what the other is thinking. They are both modest and courteous by nature and not given to acting rashly. They have a shared passion for art, although they express it in different ways. They are not naturally acquisitive, and they both have a strong sense of justice.

Realizing Steinn is watching her leaf through the folder, Hanna chooses to keep quiet. It's up to him to start talking.

"I was reading this article about van Meegeren the other day," says Steinn out of nowhere. Hanna looks at him questioningly for a moment. She knows who van Meegeren is, and while she flicks through the sketchbooks, they talk about the most infamous art forger of the twentieth century.

Han van Meegeren was Dutch and was born at the end of the nineteenth century, but he painted in the style of seventeenth-century artists like Rembrandt and Frans Hals. Art critics responded warmly to his work at first, but later they tore it apart as primitive mimicry. Van Meegeren was annoyed and set out to show that they were wrong. He decided to paint a work of art that would stand on a par with the old masters, and he made the methods and techniques of the seventeenth-century artists his own. He got hold of canvases from the period, mixed his own oils as they did then, and used special additives so the colors dried as if they were old. When the painting was finished, he baked it in an oven to dry it and then ran over the picture with a rolling pin to create cracks on the surface just like in the old paintings. He spent a full six years mastering this technique. Van Meegeren forged numerous paintings and made a lot of money selling them. He attributed his most famous forgeries to the Dutch painter Johannes Vermeer, who was alive in the seventeenth century.

"He owned fifty-two houses," Hanna comments, and Steinn snorts softly. Hanna smiles. She likes his antipathy toward accumulating wealth for the sake of it.

"Then he was arrested for treason," Hanna continues, leafing through Gudrun's pictures. "Do you remember how it all ended? One of his paintings, attributed to Vermeer, was sold to a German Nazi, who later sold it to Hermann Goering, who hid it during the war. It was found after the war, a newly discovered work of Vermeer's! The painting was traced to van Meegeren, who was arrested and charged with selling a national treasure to the enemy, which was treason. Then he painted a similar piece in prison. To prove that he could paint like Vermeer. That the painting wasn't a national treasure but a fake."

Steinn mutters something that Hanna misses.

"What I always found so strange with this," continues Hanna as she carries on leafing through, "is that his paintings aren't a bit like Vermeer's. I mean, I don't find the painting of the disciples at Emmaus remotely Vermeer-like."

"He was an oddball," says Steinn after a short silence. "A total junkie. In every respect. And during the war, Vermeer's paintings weren't accessible, so it wasn't possible to compare them. The art galleries locked up their collections down in the cellars, like we do here."

Steinn pronounces Vermeer with a soft Icelandic *v* rather than with an *f* sound, which would have been more correct given that it's a Dutch name. Hanna wonders where Steinn studied art conservation. In England maybe; they probably can't pronounce Dutch names properly there either. Or in America. Putting down the sketchbook she has just finished leafing through, she picks up another.

"Two more to go," she says. "And then those loose drawings in the box. I still haven't found the exact motif yet." She isn't as optimistic as when she started. Steinn takes out the remaining folder and quickly thumbs through it. He's clearly doing it just to speed the process up, and together they finish looking through the sketches in silence, with no success. When it's done, Steinn carefully puts everything back in its place.

Finally, he carefully lays the painting facedown on the plastic-covered table in front of Hanna. The frame is an ordinary wooden frame typical of the period, reinforced with cross slats and wooden corner wedges.

"I've taken off the outer frame—it was beyond repair," says Steinn, stroking the sides of the painting with gloved fingers. "We'll get a new frame made." They look at the brown canvas stretcher, which gives them no clues, neither a signature nor a date.

"Well, there's nothing much to see here," says Steinn. "I just wanted to show it to you. This is a homemade frame. And look, there's a tiny mistake here." He points to where two wedges have been driven into one corner, one of which is farther in than the other; the canvas stretches fractionally more on one side as a result. He turns the painting over, and, reaching above the table for the large lamp with a magnifying glass, he casts light on their project.

Hanna already feels warm, and she would rather have looked at the painting up on the easel, from a suitable distance, preferably next to Gudrun's other landscapes. She wants to sense the emotion in the work, to notice its construction, the interplay of color and brushstrokes, not examine it horizontally in front of her like a plate of food, with Steinn so close. She avoids looking at him, relieved that his hands are covered by the gloves; she has repeatedly caught herself observing his hands. He has a habit of stroking the surface of something, as if to examine it more closely and discover with his fingers what the naked eye might miss. There is a faint smell from the painting, the smell of oil paints and boiled linseed mixed with mineral oil; it's a smell Hanna likes. There's another smell, too, a whiff of something from Steinn that Hanna can't put her finger on, the smell of some substance, perhaps a cleaning fluid, thinner, turpentine, or lacquer, with a hint of soap or aftershave.

"It's in good condition, isn't it?" she says for want of something to say. Although she knows Gudrun's work very well, she has no experience of this sort of analysis; that is the conservator's specialist area.

"Yes, I suppose so," answers Steinn, glancing at her, but she doesn't immediately meet his eyes. It's as if he's looking slightly to one side, but she can't see for sure and can't very well gaze into his eyes. She looks back at the painting.

"This painting must have been listed when Gudrun sold her paintings at auction in Copenhagen to fund her time in Paris," she says.

Hanna's mind is on Steinn's eyes, she wants to scrutinize them, stare into them, and she wonders what it would be like to sink into his gaze; she has to pull herself together for a second before continuing.

"It all fits, you see. Two paintings listed for auction, both of which were sold, both with a birch motif, and one of them is fifty-by-seventy centimeters, just like this one. I was looking into it just the other day."

"Yes, this could well be," says Steinn reflectively. He's waiting for Hanna to look at the picture more carefully. When she just looks at him inquiringly, he gives a tentative cough.

"I noticed something when I first saw the painting," he explains. "Look at the sky here." He points with a gloved finger at the brushstrokes in the paint that don't match the soft banks of cloud. "These lines are coarser than in other parts of the picture and they lie directly across the clouds."

Hanna sees what he means now that he's pointed it out.

"Yes, it's obvious," she says. "In all probability there's another painting underneath. That's not uncommon, is it? Especially with a painting from this period, when painters were struggling to get a hold of canvas and oils?"

Steinn doesn't respond; he just carries on running his finger over the painting and points Hanna to other brushstrokes that cut straight across *The Birches*. For a moment they stare at the picture in silence.

"I was thinking, you see, the timing. This was painted, what—before 1940?" asks Steinn.

"Probably 1937 or '38," Hanna replies.

"But the picture underneath looks more like an abstract painting. This means that if Gudrun painted her picture over another painting, then that painting must have been virtually brand-new."

Hanna digests this. She can't work out why Steinn is being so cautious, as though he believes there's something significant here. But maybe it's just his way—to be wary until everything is clear beyond question. He is trying to tell her something without saying it straight-out, and she's not sure where he's going with this. Maybe he's intimating that it's a forgery, but she thinks that's unlikely. The painting isn't in any way amateurish, and it's in total harmony with Gudrun's style. It's a beautiful painting.

"The Danish abstract painters were beginning to work in that style by then," she says. "Obviously constructivism is older. Do you mean this is that genre?"

Steinn shakes his head. "This is more like abstract expressionism. Or, well, it could conceivably be. Perhaps in the spirit of abstract works that were painted in the wake of the CoBrA movement. That shape could be a half-moon."

Hanna waits in case he has more to add, but Steinn goes quiet.

"Or a boat," she suggests. "Harbors and boats were a popular motif back then." She peers at the painting but doesn't see a half-moon.

"I want to show you this using raking light," says Steinn patiently, and Hanna senses his underlying tenacity, which she is beginning to recognize. She knows she has to let him take the lead in this; he must be allowed to do this his way, whatever that is.

Lifting the painting off the table, Steinn carries it into a small storage area off the large workroom with Hanna following behind. He sets the painting on an easel, and, turning on an Anglepoise lamp, he adjusts it so the light falls on the painting from one side. Then he switches off the overhead fluorescent lights so that this is the only illumination in the room. The texture on the surface of the painting becomes clearer; even the tiniest unevenness casts a shadow, and Hanna sees more clearly the brushstrokes behind the subject matter of *The Birches*. Steinn runs a gloved index finger along one of these brushstrokes, diagonally from the top left-hand corner down toward the right. Undeniably, they resemble a half-moon.

"But this isn't all," says Steinn, and Hanna hears the eagerness in his voice. "Look at the trees here, the trunks I mean."

Hanna peers at the birches but doesn't notice anything in particular, just pale, gnarled birch trunks with confusing shadows on their surface. "What should I be seeing here?"

Steinn draws his finger down one of the trunks and then again just by the side of it, but Hanna can't see what he's pointing out.

"I'll show you on the computer. I've already enlarged it," says Steinn. He switches off the lamp so the shadows disappear from the surface of the painting and the copse darkens; the only light in the room is coming in from the half-open door. Steinn tries to flick the switch to bring the fluorescent lights back on but knocks into the door frame. Hanna pretends not to notice.

"Steinn is such an absentminded professor," Edda once said when he walked into the doorpost on the upper floor. "He's in a world of his own." Hanna hadn't answered. She didn't think Steinn was distracted.

They sit down at the computer in the corner out front; Hanna pulls a stool up to Steinn's chair. He has removed his gloves and is now looking for the file.

"Here we've got the light coming from the side," he says after a moment, opening up an image of the painting on the screen. The image is confusing, full of shadows, but when Steinn drags the mouse across, it becomes clear that underneath the painting of the birch copse and mountain, a shape reminiscent of a half-moon can be seen covering a large part of the picture's surface.

"Could be a boat," says Hanna again, but Steinn says nothing. Clearly he has examined this often and has his own ideas. He now magnifies one section of the picture on the screen, the one that best shows one of the birch trunks. Using the mouse, he points to the gnarled tree trunk and then to the lines next to it, straighter, not as clear, and then at an infinitesimal shadow. He searches up the next trunk and again finds straighter lines underneath and to one side. It's as if the birch had a straight trunk to begin with but has now become gnarled. Hanna can hardly believe her own eyes; this is so strange. Steinn shows her again and again; it's not easy to recognize, but once Hanna has seen it, then it's as plain as can be.

"The tree trunks have been altered," she ventures at last, unsure as to what conclusion to draw.

"Icelandic birch trees don't have straight trunks," says Steinn. "I believe there are some with straight trunks in Hallormsstadur Wood. And nowadays it's definitely possible to buy such saplings in this country. But there weren't any birches with straight trunks in Iceland in the middle of the last century."

He looks at Hanna as if waiting for confirmation of his statement. She is bewildered; this has caught her off balance, and she doesn't know what to say.

But Steinn has more up his sleeve. Closing the file of images taken with light shining from the side, he opens another one. "This is the ultraviolet version," he says. Hanna can hardly recognize the painting on the screen. She can make out various colored patches on the surface. Some are darker than others, and some sections stand out. The mountain is clear and sharp, but the trees merge together into a patchy mishmash. The sky, on the other hand, is even lighter. Hanna glances at Steinn as he peers at the screen.

"The ultraviolet light picks up the fluorescence in the colors and in the linseed varnish," he explains. "Under UV light, you can see subsequent additions or alterations made with other types of color or varnish."

"I can't make out anything from these blotches," admits Hanna. "Are you saying Gudrun started on the painting but didn't finish it until later, using different colors? That's always possible. Painters must need to renew their colors sometime and maybe don't always use the same ones." Hanna deliberately doesn't mention the possibility that the painting is a forgery, even though this is clearly what Steinn is implying. She doesn't want to be the first to say it; she wants to hear it from him.

"Conceivably," he says reluctantly after a pause. "This image isn't clear. And yet it's as if someone had altered the painting, changed the tree trunks, the mountain…" He falls silent, and Hanna realizes that he is puzzled.

"There's a substance nowadays that is a sort of mock-linseed varnish," Steinn carries on. "It appears old. Although it's actually new—it's oxidized. If a painting was covered in this sort of mock varnish, then it's a lot more difficult to see if it's been tampered with. This varnish is specially designed to deceive the UV rays."

Hanna waits for further explanation, but Steinn doesn't say anything more. He closes that file and clicks on a tab with a long list. Shifting his position, he inadvertently knocks against Hanna's knee. She slides away a fraction, still following what he's doing on the screen. He leans into the computer and scrolls up and down a long list of files.

What could be the matter with his eyes? Does he need glasses and doesn't want to use them? How can he do his job properly if his eyesight is so poor? As Hanna thinks about it more carefully, his behavior does indicate that something is wrong. It's not only that he bumps into doors; he floodlights his desk and avoids driving. He is viewed as an absentminded eccentric; she has seen it in both Edda's and Agusta's eyes. There's probably something more amiss here than plain shortsightedness. She recalls their walk through the wood. The silver ski pole that rhythmically broke the wood's silence now reminds her of another sort of stick. Hanna is so deep in thought about Steinn that the seriousness of what he is showing her fades into the background.

Steinn eventually finds what he is looking for, and now a third image of the painting lights up the screen, or at least Hanna assumes that this image is of the painting. Curved lines reminiscent of a half-moon, a shape that has nothing to do with a copse of trees or with Mount Baula, appear on the surface of the picture.

"Are you sure this is the right painting?" she asks.

"I hoped you'd ask. This is an infrared image. You're maybe familiar with the technique," he adds. "Under the oil paints is a charcoal sketch. Well, that's usually how it is. Of course, you know that in those days artists typically used charcoal to sketch out the picture before they painted it. Even pencil drawings show up on this type of image. You see, the infrared light only reflects the charcoal, not the colors or any other substances on the canvas."

Hanna looks at the image on the screen. The sharpest lines show the half-moon Steinn talked about. A half-moon drawn with straight lines, but there are a number of other less distinct lines on the surface of the picture that are difficult to make out, let alone perceive a flawless picture in them.

"There's no clear sketch of the wood here, as you can see," says Steinn. "But if you look carefully you can see lines here, look, where the birches are thickest." Steinn slides the cursor over the screen; there, with a bit of effort, lots of faint lines that could be tree trunks are just about visible.

"Do you mind if I fetch the painting? I'd like it for comparison."

Steinn gets up. "I'll go."

He pulls on the gloves lying beside the keyboard and rushes through to the storage room. He stands it up on an easel next to the computer to compare with the image on the screen and then sits back down next to Hanna. She looks hard at the real painting but can't make out any hint of the curved or diagonal lines that are so clear on the image Steinn showed her when he shone the light from one side.

She never expected the painting to be a forgery, and she's still not ready to believe it yet. The fact that there could be two paintings on the same canvas is not incredible. Artists regularly use the same canvas again if they aren't satisfied with the first attempt, and the artist's final painting is built up from many attempts. They paint over part of the picture, move one element slightly on the canvas, give the colors a different tone. Sometimes, perhaps more often in the past when colors and canvases were harder to come by, they resorted to painting over old pictures bought cheaply at flea markets or in second-hand shops. But, as Steinn pointed out, it's odd for that time for a landscape painting to be painted over an abstract painting. Abstract art was beginning to flourish in Denmark in the thirties and forties, whereas traditional landscape painting was viewed as conservative. It's virtually out of the question that Gudrun would have painted *The Birches* over an abstract work.

Steinn is a trained conservator, isn't he? With a recognized qualification in analyzing and restoring works of art. Hanna has never inquired about his background or his education; she just assumed he was qualified. Surely the art gallery wouldn't entertain employing a conservator who wasn't trained? Obviously she can't ask Steinn straight-out; she'll have to have a quiet word with Edda at an appropriate moment. Hanna isn't a trained conservator; she doesn't have the specialist, technical knowledge necessary to interpret the information these images reveal. And she is probably the only person at the gallery who knows there's something amiss with Steinn, but she's not sure what. Something seems to be up with his eyesight, but maybe Edda's right and he's just a bit absentminded.

Steinn's hand is resting on the table, curled around the mouse; his index finger is steady, poised to click if necessary. Hanna glances down at his hand, then back at the screen.

"It could be a yacht," she suggests. "A harbor scene. That fits the time frame. Harbors were popular subject matter around 1930. Or a street scene, maybe even a bridge? It's quite difficult to decipher, don't you think?"

Steinn doesn't answer. Maybe he doesn't want to be the first to voice the idea it's a forgery either. A painting that was bought from a reputable auction house in Copenhagen, a painting that in every way resembles Gudrun's work so closely and matches a painting on her auction list from that time, both in size and subject matter. How could it be a forgery? But as the UV image showed, there's undeniably something fishy about the surface painting— as though it has been altered. And if there's an abstract painting underneath, that's a strong indication something's amiss. Hanna continues to look questioningly at Steinn but is careful not to say anything. She imagines herself on the fencing piste, in the en garde stance. She can wait; she knows how to be patient.

"You're familiar with that forgery case, I suppose?" Steinn asks eventually, pulling up the UV image again while he talks. Hanna knows what he's referring to. He's going to keep on going, like a cat around a saucer of hot milk. But she's relaxed; she's got plenty of time. Steinn is referring to an extensive art forgery case investigated in Reykjavik a few years back when it came to light that there could be hundreds of forgeries in circulation.

"I found it a bit difficult to grasp the ins and outs of it. I was abroad at the time," she replies. "Did they consult the gallery or you personally?"

"No, they didn't," says Steinn dryly.

"I particularly remember one photo of a painting that was attributed to Kjarval," says Hanna, referring to Iceland's most beloved painter of the twentieth century. She's quite relieved to delay saying what's on her mind. "The sky was full of fluffy orange clouds. Nothing like Kjarval. I was really surprised."

"You wouldn't believe how amateurish some of this was," says Steinn, smiling and pulling a face. "It was a lengthy case. Extensive. The investigation took a long time. And then it all fell apart, on a formality!"

Steinn clicks the mouse sharply to enlarge part of the image on the screen. There are dark patches on a large part of the tree trunks, but they are hard to make out. Hanna looks at the painting on the easel, sees the raised brushstrokes—the ones that don't match up with the top layer of the painting. This is what put him on the scent, she thinks, picturing Steinn's fingertips running slowly and delicately across the surface of the painting.

"Of course, there are lots of ways to forge a painting," she ventures. "I didn't really follow the case very closely. Were the paintings forged from the outset?"

Steinn doesn't answer immediately but looks pensive. "Well, it kind of varied," he says at length. "Some were marginally tampered with, and others were totally repainted."

Jumping to his feet, he suddenly goes to a rack farthest back in the workroom and picks up a painting wrapped in polyethylene off the shelf. Removing the plastic, he shows her a still life painting of flowers in a vase.

"See this. Look at how the painting is structured!" Hanna senses the tension in his voice. "Who would put the vase here, right at the bottom of the picture?" he asks without waiting for an answer, and Hanna sees straightaway that there's something odd about this still life. "This was attributed to Kristin Jonsdottir."

Hanna looks at the painting. It could be, but then again maybe not. At any rate it's not typical of Kristin's dramatic flower paintings, with their dark colors and powerfully rhythmical brushstrokes. But she can't be sure. Maybe this was a painting from early in her career. Before she found her stride. It's hard to say.

"What do you think?" asks Hanna.

"It's hard to say," Steinn replies, "but look at this." He shows her Kristin Jonsdottir's signature in the bottom left-hand corner of the painting. "The original signature could have been scratched out and this one put in its place."

Hanna looks in surprise at the painting, which is oddly structured on the canvas. Suddenly it all becomes clear. A painting from an obscure artist has been taken off the canvas stretcher and cut, removing the original signature. Obviously it's not good enough to paint over the signature, which would show up on the UV image, Hanna thinks.

"Then the forger puts the painting on another canvas stretcher. It's no big deal to get a hold of an old one and paint whatever signature on it he chooses," says Steinn. "Or leave it without a signature."

"That's a bit crude," says Hanna. "Isn't that rather obvious?"

"Did you notice it before I mentioned it?" Steinn asks. She doesn't reply. Steinn is right. At first glance she didn't notice anything untoward. Steinn shrugs and wraps the painting back up.

"Don't forget that some folks who buy paintings have a limited knowledge of art. Many of them, but not all, of course. People also have faith in galleries. Who would imagine that a reputable gallery would sell a forgery? And some people simply have so much money. Owning an old master has long been a status symbol. D'you know what I saw advertised in the paper the other day?" Steinn asks in an irritated tone. "Wanted: a Kjarval painting, in beautiful colors."

"They actually specified 'in beautiful colors'?" laughs Hanna. "I wonder what colors those are."

Steinn lightens up and laughs back; their eyes meet in mutual understanding.

"That shows what the market's like, how these things can happen," he adds. "But in this forgery case, you know, this major one we were talking about, lots of paintings were forged from scratch there. Sometimes they painted on old paper or canvas. Some paintings were done on colored paper. Sometimes they used old paintings, usually by some Danish artist, and just changed the signature. The original signature was removed with sandpaper and then painted over and a new one put in its place."

While Steinn talks, Hanna wonders what they should do next, since the painting is evidently a forgery. The possibility is not so far-fetched. In the light of history, it's really rather likely. She looks at the painting on the easel and sees Steinn is watching her. This is the moment he has been waiting for, her assurance. It's so typical of Steinn to go to enormous lengths to get her to see it for herself. She realizes that her newfound conviction wouldn't be as strong if Steinn had just said it straight-out. She would have protested, thought it far-fetched.

"I still don't understand why that court case collapsed. I mean, they were all acquitted, weren't they?" says Hanna, looking at the painting. It's far from amateurish. If it's a forgery, whoever did it is no fool. She's been admiring and relishing the painting herself, and she's a qualified art historian with specialist knowledge of Gudrun's work. She finds it hard to even look at the painting now, knowing that Gudrun probably had nothing to do with it. Steinn is pensively contemplating the painting, his expression betraying his curiosity. He intends to get to the bottom of this, Hanna thinks, now realizing why he didn't bother looking at all the sketches with her. He knew it was simply a waste of time.

"Initially one man was sentenced for three of the paintings, which were attributed to Jon Stefansson. They were clearly forgeries," Steinn replies. "Then two men were charged with embezzlement and found guilty in the district court, but they took the case to a higher court and were finally sentenced by the High Court to something like two years. But the case as a whole took much longer. Over a hundred paintings were investigated, some watercolors and some oil paintings. The investigation revealed that the majority were probably forged."

"Were they charged with embezzlement?" asks Hanna. "Not just fraud?"

"Amazingly enough," says Steinn, looking at the painting, "it turned out it wasn't possible to charge them with breach of copyright just for selling fraudulent goods. They were found guilty in the district court on up to fifty counts. But then this was overturned in the High Court."

"How come?"

"Yes, well, the High Court." Steinn rubs his right eye. "They really went to town with it. The conclusion was that specialist opinions were not relevant in this case because the specialists were also the ones bringing the charges. Which wasn't even true."

Thinking like a fencer, Hanna immediately sees the next move. "So wasn't the district court verdict also dismissed and other specialists brought in? Wasn't the case reopened?"

"No," Steinn answers, and they fall silent.

Hanna is disturbed. She followed the case at the time, but being abroad meant she soon forgot about it. Now she reproaches herself for her indifference.

"It was one of the most costly and lengthy cases in Icelandic legal history, and it was a complete fiasco," Steinn adds, frowning. "Just petered out. And the paintings went straight back into circulation." There's a hint of irritation in his voice, yet Steinn generally doesn't get annoyed at anything.

"Back in circulation!" Hanna doesn't believe him. "That can't be right."

Steinn nods emphatically. "The law doesn't prevent it."

Hanna looks back at *The Birches*. Steinn is keen to uncover the truth about this painting. He has been living here and working in the arts, and over recent years he has witnessed justice not being done. Of course it's intolerable. Steinn is a man who never gives in. Hanna can see herself getting involved in this with him; although the task is far from what she imagined when she took the job as director of the Annexe.

"We need to take a closer look at the ownership history," Steinn says. "Kristin mentioned that Elisabet bought the painting at an auction of Holst's estate, but that doesn't ring true. I've asked around."

Hanna looks at him thoughtfully. "Is that so? Did she say that?" Frowning, she tries to remember what Kristin said at that meeting. Steinn doesn't wait while she's thinking.

"It doesn't matter what she said. The point is that Elisabet bought the painting at a different auction house from the one who auctioned the slaughterer's estate. That means that someone else bought the painting from his estate and then put it back up for auction. A few months later. With a different auction house."

"Oh," says Hanna.

"We need to find the missing link—whoever bought the painting at the first auction. Maybe it was a totally different price then. It's a pain that auction houses don't give out that kind of information."

"Don't they? Why not?"

Steinn is lost in thought and doesn't respond, so she doesn't push it for now. She must be able to find a way forward now that he's so pessimistic.

The silence between them deepens. Hanna senses his eyes resting on her as though he wants to say something but can't bring himself to. Not knowing what he is thinking, she starts to feel uncomfortable but can't ask him straight-out. It's just the way he is. They've only worked together for three weeks, and their private lives have never come up in conversation. Their friendship is purely professional, although it's also genuine. They don't know one another well enough for her to ask what's the matter, what he wants. She will have to work that out for herself, like she worked out that the painting is likely to be a forgery, even though neither of them has said as much out loud.

She looks at the painting on the easel, at the image on the computer screen, at Steinn's hand on the mouse. Thinking about how Steinn bumped into the doorpost just now, how he leaned forward over the computer screen, how he knocked her knee, it finally dawns on her what this is all about. She suddenly sees his helpfulness in a new light, his friendliness and kindness and the encouragement he's given her on a daily basis since she joined.

Now it's her turn. Steinn needs her support. He can't do this on his own, and he's also frightened about something, maybe losing his sight or not being able to do his job properly any longer.

Of course, Hanna's specialist knowledge of Gudrun's paintings will play a big part in this. Right from the first day, Steinn realized that they would be ideal brothers in arms. Of course I'll help you, she thinks. We're in this together. And what you fear, whatever that is, I'll be there for you. Nodding her head, she sees his relief. He turns back to the computer.

"Here, look at this. Do you remember? The UV image here shows best of all that something has clearly been tampered with."

Hanna sits next to him, and now she doesn't worry about sitting close; in this moment they are comrades. All we need now is to swear an oath, she says to herself, to slice our palms and mingle our blood. She smiles to herself. Steinn would look good with a sword.

"I need to get an X-ray," he says. "An X-ray might show more clearly what's underneath, but it's time-consuming. To do this sort of thing properly, we'd really need to send it abroad. Maybe I can sort something out over here. I'll look into it. If it becomes apparent that there's an abstract painting underneath this landscape, then it's almost certainly a forgery."

For a moment Steinn hesitates; then, taking a deep breath, he begins talking uncharacteristically fast.

"Then we might just consider whether we should simply wash off the whole of the upper layer." He breathes out again as if he'd been holding his breath for some time, and Hanna is startled. There it is. What he'd been thinking about all the while. This is what he wants.

"Wash off the entire top layer? But what about Gudrun's landscape? What will happen to that?" Steinn looks at Hanna and then it dawns on her. The likelihood is there is no landscape of Gudrun's on this canvas.

Steinn is sure of his case. Now that they've started on this journey there's no turning back. They have to go the whole way, to see it through. In her head she draws her foil out of its sheath, lifts it up, and holds it there at the ready against an unseen enemy.

It's her job to confirm his conclusions, to examine the images on the screen more carefully, alongside the painting on the easel. It's up to her to write the report—she's worried about the response it will trigger, she's scared to hear something she doesn't want to hear. Is that why she doesn't ask Steinn about his eyesight? She sits still. She wasn't expecting this.

Steinn turns the computer off. Hanna forces herself to move, to stand up. Walking over to the painting, Hanna gazes at the birch grove, as if she's trying to reach out through time and space and make contact with Gudrun. With the person who painted this landscape. The painting hasn't changed. The mountain is immovable, the birch trees are finely nuanced, the trunks are light and bright, and colors dance on the forest floor. Unchanged, yet not the same as it was. With a deep sense of disappointment, Hanna breathes in quickly and turns around, to Steinn. He's standing there, waiting.

3

INTERNATIONAL BUSINESS CONFERENCE
MOSCOW, 2004

Hrafn pulls his hands as far as he can up into his jacket sleeves. He has broad, meaty hands, like soft paws, which he tries to hide by wearing suits specially tailored for him, with sleeves just long enough to disguise the size of his hands. He is ashamed of them and thinks they bear false witness to years of toil as a workman, a farmer, or a sailor. Hrafn has never lifted his hands in manual labor; he hasn't tilled the soil, let alone hauled a fish from the sea. The work his fingers recognize is tapping a computer keyboard, and his palm fits comfortably around a mouse. He is proud of never having had to do manual labor, but these hands run in the family, inherited from earlier generations, an inheritance Hrafn has no use for in his line of work.

He is sitting in an avant-garde conference hall in a new building in Moscow. The seats are wine red, wide, and plush, the color faintly reminiscent of old political leanings. The hall is crowded, primarily with men in suits of varying shades of gray. Hrafn has his computer open on the swivel table attached to his seat, reading the business pages of the English newspapers while the words of the Icelandic minister go in one ear and out the other.

"As the minister for fisheries and agriculture it is a great pleasure for me to address this international business conference here in Moscow," announces the minister. "For many decades, Russia and Iceland have enjoyed good business relations," he continues. "In previous years, these relations were largely confined to fish processing, the sale of herring, fishing tackle, and equipment, but nowadays we have business deals springing up in many spheres. Today we not only have representatives of the Icelandic fishing industry, but also stakeholders of large telecommunications and pharmaceutical corporations. We have representatives from Icelandic banks and, last but not least, up-and-coming young musicians and artists."

The fisheries minister glances over the crowded hall, his eyes flitting from one delegate to another; they rest briefly on Hrafn before he returns to his speech. "Icelandic fisheries are different from those of other countries," he says proudly. "Different in the sense that they do not enjoy public funding. They are privately run."

And so his speech goes on. Hrafn looks around the hall. He knows some of the Icelanders here; he has personal connections with the Icelandic visual arts and regularly attends arts events in Reykjavik, so he recognizes many faces among the artists. Hrafn is an only child who inherited a collection of paintings from his father, Arni, who was a shipowner, passionately patriotic, with a heart of gold and a fondness for drink. Arni was a hands-on man; he knew all his employees and their families personally and could address their children by name.

It annoyed Hrafn to listen to his father singing the praises of his workers and his country, singing patriotic songs in a haze of bluish smoke with his London Docks cigar in one hand and a glass of cognac in the other, sitting under a painting by Gunnlaugur Scheving of sailors battling a storm. He felt his father's attitude belonged to a bygone age.

Arni was a generous man who loved the arts and knew how to enjoy the good things of life, but in his later years, his business went into decline and he lacked the drive to expand or to update his assets. He didn't keep abreast of developments in his field; he just stuck with tried-and-trusted methods. After his death, Hrafn totally turned the business around, got it back up again, and tripled its turnover.

The paintings Arni had collected were a haphazard selection of works by amateurs and professional artists—pictures of the harbor, townscapes of Reykjavik, landscapes, and sentimental paintings of sunsets. Arni bought paintings from most of the people who knocked on his door. In his eyes, artists' contributions formed an important part of the nation's self-image. These men stood side by side with Arni in the struggle to achieve a decent life for an independent nation. Men, for there were no women who knocked on Arni's door; he was not that progressive.

After his father's death, Hrafn had experts value the collection; he got rid of the sunsets but held on to the cultural heritage. In his eyes, the paintings are a financial investment. Hrafn is not given to patriotic feelings. He knows his art collection inside out; he has made it his business to know the life's work of the most highly respected painters and the price their works will fetch. He knows which periods are the most sought after, where the missing links in the chain are, and where the market has been saturated. Hrafn rates his paintings according to their value; the most valuable ones are in storage. He collects works almost exclusively by deceased artists.

Hrafn feels his phone vibrate in his breast pocket. He recognizes the number. He has been in discussion with Kristin, the director of the Reykjavik gallery, recently. She is constantly networking in the private sector for financial support, both for one-off exhibitions and ongoing projects, and one of her pet projects is to get rid of the entrance fee. So far he has avoided committing himself, but now he needs to make a decision, either to refuse or agree to support her project, but he still has not made up his mind. He doesn't pick up. The gallery is not his priority, and Kristin will have to wait for the moment; he will talk to her later. Hrafn is keen to support the gallery financially, but he is not sure he wants to fork out the sum she's after and not get anything tangible in return.

Hrafn views paintings through the eye of common sense and not from the heart as his father did. He is not at all interested in the artists here at the conference, paid for by the state with the aim of enhancing his country's image abroad and showing that Iceland is a player on the international stage. He has no interest in art. Modern art is meaningless to him; he doesn't understand it and doesn't see what drives these artists.

Having looked over the stock market situation, Hrafn subtly tilts his computer screen toward him and opens up the web page of a Copenhagen auction house. Dealing in paintings is his private business. Hrafn keeps a regular eye on the web pages of auction houses in London and Copenhagen, and he wants to see which paintings have come up for auction since the previous evening.

He spots Vasiliy Ivanov Gubin's balding head two rows in front; Vasya, his father's old business colleague. His father, Arni, and Vasya were best friends, and Hrafn rarely feels as close to his father as when he meets Vasya, who is like a kindly uncle to him. Vasya reminds him of his father's good points: courtesy, hospitality, friendship, and compassion for his fellow men. On the other side of the hall he spots Stanislav Petrov's rosy, youthful face—his contact in the pharmaceutical company, whom he wants to clinch a deal with during this trip. Hrafn wants more shares and he needs Stanislav's support.

"Icelanders own more mobile phones per capita than any other nation," the minister continues. Hrafn doesn't listen to him but quickly runs his eyes down the auction house web page. Some paintings have been added; one of them seems familiar. He looks at it more closely; the artist is listed as unknown. He tries to work out who it could be. Enlarging some of the detail on the screen, he looks carefully at the brushstrokes, but he can't be sure. It's a landscape painting, probably Danish but could be Icelandic. Or a painting by some Icelandic artist who trained in Denmark. He checks the value and the work's origins. The value is very low and the ownership history seems convincing; the painting has been in the same family for years. The auction is just about to begin, and he puts in a generous bid. He could be onto something. A faint scent of perfume stirs his senses; behind him sits the owner of the gallery where the art side of this business conference is housed.

She wears her dyed blonde hair up in a plait, and her lips are bright red. Hrafn has not been introduced to her, but the minister pointed her out to him before the meeting. "Mariya Kovaleva," he'd said. "One of the wealthiest women in Russia today." Hrafn's interest had been aroused and he'd resolved to talk to her before the day was out.

"I think we can say without a doubt that Icelandic business is booming like never before," the minister says in closing. Hrafn glances back at his screen; there's something about this painting that interests him.

There is a dinner at the Hotel Kosmopolitan that evening, in a restaurant on the twenty-fifth floor with a view over the city. Hrafn is sitting next to Mariya Kovaleva and a young woman called Larisa, who seems to be her personal assistant. Stanislav is also at the table, along with the minister, two bankers, and their wives. It's a veritable banquet, and there are lavish quantities of food and drink. Hrafn is used to this sort of thing and he knows how to manage an event like this; he drinks mineral water and eats little. He observes the others around the table who do not employ quite the same table manners as he does. He is a polite man, modest by nature and not given to pushing himself forward. His open face has a classic bone structure; he has a sportsman's build and a rare smile. He is accustomed to attracting looks from both men and women no matter where he is. But he is not talkative, and this evening he only talks to Stanislav or remains silent. He pays attention to the conversation around the table without taking part. From time to time he catches Larisa's eye or smiles at Mariya Kovaleva across the large round table, raising his glass to a toast.

His fellow diners have been celebrating since the opening at Mariya Kovaleva's gallery this afternoon. The gallery is enormous; it is in a new building in the city center right next to the

Pushkin Museum. It currently houses an exhibit of contemporary Russian artists alongside Icelandic artists. Many delegates from the conference attended the opening, but Hrafn talked almost exclusively to Vasya. Not about business, but about the family. Hrafn told him he was expecting his third child. Vasya talked about his wife's illness. Hrafn asked if there was anything he could do, offered to cover the medical costs at a private clinic in America, but Vasya refused.

The evening is wearing on, and the banker's wife sitting next to Hrafn is tired and tipsy. She has tried various topics of conversation with Hrafn with little success before discovering that he is a horseman. They have something in common. Hrafn listens politely as she talks about her horses and her riding.

"So you obviously don't eat horse meat, do you?" she asks, leaning in toward him, somewhat red-eyed with tousled hair and circles under her eyes. Her husband watches her out of the corner of his eye. But Hrafn is not interested in this woman or in talking to her about horses; he is contemplating moving so he can talk to Mariya and Larisa.

"Only fillet," he says, pushing his chair from the table in order to extricate himself from this gathering and move away. He hears the banker's wife repeating his words to her husband.

"He's hardly likely to eat his own horses," replies the husband, and then their words are drowned out in the general babble.

"Mr. Arnason? Mr. Arnason!" Mariya calls to him, and Hrafn walks over to her and takes her outstretched hand. She shakes his hand warmly, too warmly in Hrafn's view, and too long. He is curious but says nothing.

"This is Larisa," says Mariya without further explanation. "We're off to a private party. Come and join us." At this Larisa obediently gets up from the table, up from the dessert, profiteroles—choux pastry filled with whipped cream—which are just being served. The cream puffs are shaped like swans, and Mariya reaches out for one, biting off its head and smiling up at Hrafn.

"I hear you're an art collector," she says in her stiff English with a marked accent, stuffing the remains of the swan into her mouth. "The minister told me. I must show you my private collection."

Hrafn allows himself to be led away from the table without saying good-bye to his fellow diners, who are still drinking; he makes do with patting Stanislav lightly on the shoulder. He is relieved to get away; he finds eating and drinking with people he has no interest in getting to know a waste of time. He has already got all he needs in life. But he can't resist a business opportunity and is sure that getting to know Mariya, or Masha as she has asked him to call her, will provide new breaks into the Russian market, although he doesn't yet know what sort. She is well connected at any rate.

On their way out Masha signals to two men who are about to follow them. Speaking in undertones, she says something in Russian, and they shake their heads but let the matter drop. They look like bodyguards. Larisa takes Hrafn's arm and smiles without saying anything. She is blonde with brown eyes and has a dimple in her heart-shaped face. They go out of the back entrance and into a black car waiting there; the windows are tinted.

Hrafn loses his sense of direction almost immediately and doesn't know where they are. For a second he sees lit-up buildings reflected in the Moscow River, *Reka Moskva*, then for some time the car winds its way along poorly lit back streets. Hrafn feels Larisa's hand resting gently on his knee. He doesn't react; he is waiting to see how this will turn out. The car comes to a standstill outside a block of flats on a side street. Mariya and Larisa quickly jump out, and Hrafn follows them. The car glides away, virtually silent. Masha gets out her key, which she slips into the lock, and opens the door to the main entrance with a flourish. Once inside, they don't go into the luxury flat Hrafn sees through an open door off the richly carpeted hallway, but straight up to the next floor. Again Masha opens up with the key. There is some coming and going down below, and they hear someone rushing toward the stairs. Masha calls something down in Russian, and the footsteps fade away again.

They enter a darkened room with parquet flooring. Hrafn picks out a faint smell of oil paints and linseed oil varnish, as though they've come into an artist's studio. When Larisa switches on the light, the sheer volume of paintings on the walls takes him by surprise. The sliding doors between the large, spacious rooms are open, rooms that are like small exhibition spaces in a gallery. Hrafn looks twice at Larisa. She has taken off the jacket she wore over her cocktail dress; the dress is beautiful, but not as beautiful as she is. He concentrates on the paintings on the walls; he is familiar with the subject matter— Russian landscapes in nineteenth-century style. Hrafn points to one of them.

"Shishkin?" he asks, naming the one Russian painter that comes to mind. Shishkin was around in the nineteenth century, and his paintings are among the more expensive ones on the market. Smiling, Larisa nods. Together they walk through three large rooms full of paintings; Larisa lets their art speak for itself. Hrafn has never seen a private collection on par with this. The most famous artists in history. Rembrandt, Velazquez, Goya, Matisse, Picasso. The collection is clearly extraordinarily valuable and to invite him in is most unusual. Someone who owns a collection like this would hardly be inclined to advertise the fact to a stranger, and Hrafn guesses that there are security guards on the lower floor.

Masha has disappeared. Larisa settles down on a leather sofa over in the far corner and invites him to come and sit next to her, but Hrafn declines. She is open about what she has in mind, but he has never cheated on his wife. In his eyes, cheating is a sign of instability and immaturity. Nor does he trust business colleagues who are unfaithful to their wives. Larisa accepts his refusal with exceptional courtesy, as though nothing had happened. She simply gets up, leads the way back, and slips her jacket back on without him noticing.

"This is the largest private collection of nineteenth-century Russian paintings inside Russia," says Larisa as she takes a bottle of champagne from the table and pours them each a glass. Hrafn takes the glass but does not drink. He sees. Sees that Mariya is rich and powerful—she has servants, bodyguards, refined and educated escorts on her payroll—and Larisa is an art historian. What's Mariya's game?

Hrafn smiles at Larisa and thanks her for inviting him. It was an honor to view this beautiful and remarkable collection. But he must be off now; he has a number of taxing meetings ahead of him tomorrow. Larisa asks him to wait a moment, then disappears. Shortly after a man dressed in black comes and escorts Hrafn to the door. The same black car is waiting for him out on the street. The man in black hurries Hrafn out and into the car as if a hidden marksman were around the corner, waiting for his moment.

4

A WALK IN THE ALPS
REYKJAVIK, CURRENT DAY

Hanna intends to fulfill her promise to Steinn and call Denmark today; he is not keen on this sort of phone call. She isn't entirely sure which approach to take with the auction house in Copenhagen where Elisabet Valsdottir bought *The Birches*, artist currently unknown, but she intends to get what she needs. Steinn is tenacious, she thinks to herself, but I don't give up so easily either.

They both want to know who put *The Birches* up for auction, who profited nearly eight million Icelandic kronur from its sale. Hanna will need to be cunning but courteous; she must sheath her foil. Auction houses are invariably on their guard. There is always someone who is trying to get forged paintings onto the market. She doesn't want to be too pushy and have the person on the other end get defensive as a result.

Steinn is still waiting for the X-rays. He knows someone who works in the radiology department at the hospital, but he has not found time to X-ray the painting yet. In the meantime, they will have to look for clues elsewhere by tracing the painting's history, looking for inconsistencies, something that doesn't ring true.

Finally Hanna takes the plunge and dials the number. She starts off trying to make do with her high school Danish in the hopes that any Dane would be pleased to hear an Icelander trying to speak Danish. The auction house's phone number is on the home page; she has the website open in front of her on the screen as she dials.

"Vabeha?"

The voice on the other end is impatient, and Hanna decides straightaway not to attempt any further Danish and switches over to English. That works better, and the voice softens very slightly.

"The painting was attributed to the Icelandic painter Gudrun Johannsdottir," she repeats in English, but the man at the auction house is not really listening. Hanna tries her best to pronounce the name in some sort of international way that could be understood anywhere. "Gudrun Johannsdottir." She pronounces the *j* as *dj* as she would in English. "Djo-hanns-dot-tir," she repeats, trying to remain as friendly and polite as she can. She feels that a member of staff at the auction house should recognize the name. Gudrun was very much a key player among Icelandic painters and exhibited a lot abroad. Mostly in Paris but also in Scandinavia. Evidently before this man's time, because he now asks her to spell the name. In her head Hanna quickly tries to find words to match the letters in Gudrun's name while spelling it correctly. "*G* as in George. *U* as in…" She falls silent for a moment. *U* as in what, an English or a Danish word? "*U* as in under," she says hesitantly, but the message seems to transmit across the sea. "*D* as in David." She continues to spell Gudrun's name out in full. "And *dottir* like the Danish word *datter*," she says finally, but the man on the other end doesn't understand what she means and so she has to spell *dottir*, daughter, as well.

"And when was the painting purchased?" The man on the other end is clearly jotting down her inquiry about the painting's ownership history. He is probably just someone who answers the phone; at least that's how he comes across. Judging by the range of items on offer on their website, it is a big auction house that operates on a considerable scale—it is hardly likely the staff are all specialist art historians. The auction house has much more than paintings on offer, and Hanna looks through the selection of goods for sale while she is talking. The collectors' pages remind her of the Duke of Berry's treasures. She is attracted by a Russian damask doll, embroidered with a crown and a monogram. It costs around one hundred thousand Icelandic kronur. Someone has bid nearly fifty thousand. While she is answering the man's questions, Hanna tries to imagine what sort of person buys these things.

"I think it was purchased just before New Year's, but I don't have an exact date," she says. She can hear the keyboard tapping. He is searching. Hanna clicks on a picture of a decorative Chinese tree with flowers and leaves made of valuable stones. The tree is set to go for around forty thousand Icelandic kronur. However, a monk's figurine carved from wood from the seventeenth century is valued at well over a hundred thousand. Would she give Frederico something like that for Christmas if they were rich? She smiles to herself until she remembers. Depending on whether they have another Christmas together.

"I need to look into this more," says the voice on the phone. "If you give me your number I'll call you later in the week."

Hanging up, Hanna senses nothing will come of it. She has to admit that Steinn is right; information of this sort is not handed out on a plate. But now she must get her brain in gear for the next project. She has invited four artists to take part in her landscape exhibition in the spring and has asked them to meet here in the Annexe. She is curious to see how they get along.

Creating works of art is addictive, something well known to artists who have not had the opportunity to produce any art for some time. They see their creative urge, find some other outlet, in the kitchen, the garden, in DIY around the house, having another baby, or in being generally surly. This urge is like a disability, Hanna thinks to herself as she stands welcoming the artists in the Annexe's exhibition room. They all have it, no matter what their age or what form it takes. They all simply want to see their art come into being. To feel an idea taking shape, see it develop and then emerge into the world. There is fulfillment in seeing your ideas coming to fruition. Luxury. Maybe this is why artists repeatedly reconcile themselves to working unpaid, working on their art in their spare time and all for this: to see their art come alive.

The painter, Haraldur, keeps some distance from the others, his expression at once proud and embittered. He stands erect, still in his overcoat and woolen hat, shuffling his feet as if he doesn't know what to do with himself. Jon Egilsson is relaxed, his soft features have success written all over them, and he has the good-natured appearance of a man who lives a comfortable life. His overcoat is casually draped over his arm, and something about his manner says that he has lived abroad for many years.

They were born the same year but belong to different generations of artists. Both were fascinated by schools of art around the middle of the previous century, and both attracted attention early on. Haraldur for his huge abstract paintings, which are on show in banks, public buildings, and companies around the country. Jon for his sculptures, performances, and conceptual art. He has never painted a picture. He has lived in Belgium for almost his entire career. Haraldur stuck with abstract art right up to the seventies and then began to lean toward landscape painting. Now he paints lyrical landscapes almost exclusively. As an artist he portrays tenderness and gentleness, those sides of Icelandic nature that are often overshadowed by the magnificent and awe-inspiringly beautiful, and yet are so important to us. Beneath his gruff exterior lies a genuine artist, a passionate painter who has fallen foul of the present day, and that's a shame, Hanna thinks to herself. But she is fed up with his continual mistrust. The hardest part will be getting Haraldur to work with the others; Jon will not be a problem.

Leifur Finnson is from the youngest generation of artists, consumed with burning ambition, passion, and joy at creating his art. He only recently graduated from the Icelandic Academy of Arts and so is rather excited to be asked to take part in an exhibition at the municipal gallery. Anselma is a young German artist whose career she has followed over recent years, and Hanna is pleased to be able to give her this opportunity here. Anselma is calm, experienced, and does not have the expectations that Leifur has. She has seen competition on the international stage and produces her own brand of art and takes the consequences with equanimity.

Agusta told Hanna about Leifur's background and his battle to become an artist; it sounded like a tale from the old days, of an unworldly romantic who walks alone, without a care for wealth or security. "He's the son of a master carpenter and a primary school teacher, and his parents are very ordinary middle-class people," said Agusta. "But they were totally against him going to the Arts Academy. His father wanted him to take over the family business because Leifur is a talented carpenter. And that's proved very useful to him and to many others at the Academy. His parents don't see any future in studying art. So in order to instill a bit of discipline, even though he's no longer a child, they decided that if he studied at the Academy he would have to fend for himself entirely. So he left home the minute he got a place there. Everyone was against him apart from his girlfriend, who has stood by him like a rock," said Agusta. "Even his friends didn't understand him—rather than go out partying he wanted to stay at home and create his sculptures."

Hanna looks at Leifur's hands fiddling with a pencil, dirt under his nails, strong supple hands, with a carved silver ring on his wedding finger.

"Lilja told me," said Agusta. "She was his lecturer. There was a risk of him giving up in the first semester because he didn't fit in with the group. He hadn't ever gone to an exhibition, you see, didn't know any artists, and had a different taste in music. He dressed differently. He didn't believe in himself and didn't think he would make it, but Lilja managed to get him to change his mind. Nevertheless, it wasn't until the final semester that he blossomed, when he created that installation from wood, the one that I was telling you about."

Hanna was thrilled by Leifur's artworks the minute she saw pictures of them. She doesn't have a clue what he intends to do in this exhibit, but in her eyes all his works are modern-day landscapes that blend with the city and create a background for its life. He makes sculptures that flow through the exhibition space. Using discarded building materials, roofing felt, rusty corrugated iron, wooden offcuts, glass, anything that happens to be available when a house is demolished, or discarded materials from a newly built house, he creates a richly nuanced composition of colors and textures.

"He barely speaks to his parents even now," said Agusta, and Hanna lets out a sigh at the thought, wishing that she had the money to pay Leifur a decent sum for his work, rather than just cover the cost of the raw materials. And how is he going to sell such large installations that you cannot store or build over again? Fortunately, he is still too young to worry about whether his work will sell; he is unrealistic and optimistic and this allows him to think big. Maybe he's one of those who won't give up, she thinks. One of those who keeps going until he's able to live from his art.

Hanna'd had to coax Haraldur to take part. It was not until they had been talking for some time about various Icelandic and foreign painters that he reluctantly agreed to join in. He would have agreed immediately to an exhibition in the main gallery, but the Annexe is another matter altogether. The Annexe is an avant-garde exhibition space that does not give paintings precedence over other media. Haraldur harbors a deep mistrust for such movements. He has very little confidence in Hanna, but the fact that his paintings have not been seen on the gallery's walls for decades overcame his artistic reservations about the validity of this exhibition.

This is like religion, Hanna thinks to herself. Doesn't narrow-mindedness contradict the very spirit of art? Haraldur doesn't believe that any of the younger generation have a genuine interest in his art. Let alone these youngsters, she thinks, looking at Leifur and Anselma. Haraldur would be surprised if he knew how open these two actually were to his art. He projects his own narrow-mindedness onto others.

The two older men take a sideways glance at the young ones, Jon out of curiosity, Haraldur with a distinct look of disdain. Collaboration is not in his nature, not because he is stubborn or myopic—working with others, which is common among contemporary artists, is simply alien to him.

"Well now," Hanna begins. "Welcome."

Mentally she slips into fencing mode, into the starting position. She feels the heaviness in her feet, the balance in her core, her body full of energy in readiness; the others are looking at her, waiting.

"Nice to see you all," she says calmly, ready to go into defense or attack mode. "We're here today to have a chat. Sort of, informally, to get to know one another. Well, maybe you've not met, so let me introduce you," she says, and from the introductions it turns out that they know one another, apart from Anselma and Haraldur. Jon taught Leifur at the Academy of Arts, and Leifur did some carpentry for the gallery that occasionally exhibits Haraldur's work. Jon is the friendliest of them all. He has the most experience, not only in art, but also in the interpersonal relations that this entails.

"How is the gallery going to go about this?" asks Leifur. "You see, I was thinking of a booklet and pictures and so on. And the exhibition space? I think you were talking about some artwork in public spaces, weren't you?"

Hanna has already visited them individually and explained that they are free to do as they please, either in the Annexe or in a public space, which they could discuss with the local authorities.

"I know for sure that we'll have Haraldur's paintings in this room here," says Hanna, hoping Haraldur will say something. But Haraldur merely stands there silently, his arms folded across his chest—he has no intention of speaking to these youngsters or to Hanna. "In other respects we don't know what the exhibit will be like," she adds. "I think it will be exciting to have new pieces, but that isn't by any means a stipulation. Not at all," she adds, looking toward Haraldur. "What I have in mind is to display a variety of ideas about landscape in contemporary arts, on a small scale, a variety where every voice can be heard. Obviously, landscape is a very broad concept."

Leifur nods his head. His eyes are a beautiful green-brown with golden flecks. His dark unruly hair tumbles over his forehead.

"You can link the concept of landscape with almost anything at all," says Hanna. "You interpret it as you wish, naturally. Landscape is the underlying theme of the exhibition and I'll write about it in the program, but you are free to do what you want. You don't need to take the concept literally," she says more to herself than to the others.

Not necessarily, she thinks, and yet in her mind's eye she pictures a mountain. The light falling on it. The colors. The proportions of the mountain, the sky, and the sea. Somewhere these elements come together perfectly. Maybe in one of Ruisdael's paintings. If Vermeer had painted a landscape with mountains, it would have been the consummate landscape painting. Cezanne got close to it. The tenderness of Haraldur's paintings. The mountains back home in Leirhofn. *The Birches* springs to mind, and yet again she wonders who did this beautiful painting, if it wasn't Gudrun.

"It's been said that in every age societies look within and reveal how they view the world through the landscape paintings of their artists," says Hanna. "I think that from our own countryside we should be able to come up with something about ourselves, our worldview, and our society, and express that through images of the Icelandic landscape. What I'm saying is just an attempt to see things in a larger context. Like Petrarch." Hanna looks at Jon and Haraldur. Haraldur is nodding, while Jon looks blank.

"Francesco Petrarch was born in Italy in the fourteenth century, but as the fates would have it he grew up and studied in France. He became famous for his writings and traveled widely in Europe. Among other things he collected old manuscripts and he is seen as one of the initiators of the Renaissance in Italy. Petrarch is also remembered in history for his remarkable accounts of landscapes and has been called Petrarca Alpinista, the first mountaineer. It was not common in his day to go hiking for pleasure, but he climbed Mont Ventoux in southern France with the sole aim of admiring the view. When he had reached the summit, he looked all around in awe and wonder, and the story goes that he opened one of Saint Augustine's sacred writings from the fourth century, which he was particularly fond of. And it so happened that he opened it at the page that says man should look within rather than wonder at the glory of nature. And naturally Petrarch was filled with remorse," Hanna explains. "As if he'd made a major mistake. I wanted to tell you this tale because Petrarch finds himself in such an exciting position in this story. Should he look out or in, forward or to the past? He is at a turning point. Which way are we going to look?"

Hanna stops talking. Outside the window the bluish hues of the morning give way to white daylight. The sidewalk is dark gray where the underground hot water pipes have thawed the snow; the square is white. It's snowing heavily, large wet flakes. Hanna sees that she is losing Haraldur to the snowfall.

"I don't quite get these landscape ideas of yours," says Leifur, suddenly irritated by the account of a long-dead Italian poet to whom he cannot relate. "I'm no landscape painter. Nor am I keen on exhibitions where the curator has the main say."

"You have a completely free hand in this," Hanna repeats, sensing how her story has backfired, as if the thought she was trying to get across has turned against her and instead of being liberating has come over as reactionary. "What I really want to hear from you as soon as possible are your ideas. Maybe you don't have any ideas right now, but we can speak again later."

Leifur moves off a few paces, trying to keep himself in check. Hanna decides to give him time to calm down and says nothing. Walking toward the window, he takes his hands out of his pockets; his fists are no longer clenched. He turns his back to them as he talks.

"Yeah, well, of course I don't know what I'm going to do. I don't think that far ahead. Still, I'd be up for doing something that kind of evolves. I've got loads of junk in a friend's garage he wants to get rid of."

Hanna nods. She doesn't know whether Leifur has staged this little scene to get attention, and she isn't bothered either way, just mumbles something encouraging and avoids meeting Haraldur's eye. Haraldur walked off toward the gallery the minute Leifur mentioned the junk in the garage, but now he turns around and looks accusingly at Hanna. That's where he wants to be, Hanna thinks to herself. Inside the gallery. Not here in this experimental space.

"An exhibition like this is an interactive process," she says, immediately seeing from Haraldur's expression that her choice of words goes right against the grain. In his opinion terms like "interactive process" have nothing in common with art. She could kick herself.

"We'll find a way that's acceptable to all," she says at last, looking straight at Haraldur, who looks back at her angrily. In the end, he cannot keep silent.

"Junk in the garage!" He looks at Jon and Hanna as if these words say it all, turns on his heel, and storms out. Agusta looks at Hanna.

"Should I go after him?" she asks with a worried look, but Hanna shakes her head.

"He'll come around," she says and smiles at Leifur. "He'll see the light yet."

Leifur does not smile back. They are not on the same side. But Hanna sees the oppositions the exhibition will revolve around, and that pleases her. This incident confirms where these two are coming from, and that is no surprise to Hanna.

It will be difficult to bridge the gap between these artists, but she is convinced that it will work, from the point of view of their artwork at least, although it is unlikely that it will spark a friendship between Leifur and Haraldur.

Closing the computer that has been sitting open on the floor all the while, Anselma finally begins speaking in a nasal voice. From her experience with Dutch and German artists Hanna knows that the time has come to discuss the practicalities.

"How is it with the town council?" asks Anselma in her slightly broken Icelandic. "Isn't there yet another new committee for culture?"

In the past year or so the civic authorities have repeatedly changed and so has the personnel on the various municipal bodies as a result. Hanna hears the familiar tone of resignation in Anselma's voice, the weariness of someone who constantly sees problems instead of possibilities, but she doesn't let it get to her. Anselma doesn't know it yet, but thanks to her job in Amsterdam, Hanna is a past master at sitting on committees and fighting her corner. Anselma will soon come to realize this. Mentally moving into the resting position, Hanna smiles at her; she will take this parry lightly. There's an almost tangible release of tension from the room following Haraldur's exit, and she becomes even more determined to have him involved, come what may.

5

IN THE FOREGROUND

E-mails have been flying back and forth between Hanna and her friends since she arrived in the country. Yet they still have not found an evening that suits them all, so they've settled on meeting for lunch today instead. Even then, only three of them, Hanna, Gudny, and Laufey, are able to make it to the vegetarian restaurant downtown.

That morning Hanna goes to the national library in search of information on Christian Holst's art collection, the butcher who owned *The Birches* for so many years. She does not find anything about Holst but discovers a number of things about Elisabeth Hansen, the Danish art collector whose paintings were the jewel in Holst's collection.

Reading the description of Elisabeth Hansen, with her red hair and lively manner, Hanna is reminded of a letter by Gudrun Johannsdottir that she found in the gallery's archives. It was written in 1939 to a good friend of Gudrun's who was living in Italy at the time. In the letter Gudrun describes the evening she and her friend Sigfus Gunnarsson visited Elisabeth

Hansen. Elisabeth used to hold an open house one evening a week with free food. These events were frequented by Danish abstract painters, some of whom later became part of the CoBrA movement. Sigfus was among them, and Elisabeth made him very welcome but cold-shouldered Gudrun all evening.

Gudrun mentions in the letter that Sigfus had sold a painting to Elisabeth that same evening. Where might this picture be and what sort of painting was it? Hanna thinks to herself, huddled over the books. If Sigfus had sold Elisabeth a painting then it probably went to the butcher, as he bought up virtually her whole collection.

After a bit of searching Hanna finally turns up something about the butcher in a book about Danish abstract painters. It emerges that at the end of his life, Christian Holst gave nearly all his CoBrA paintings to an art gallery on Jutland. Maybe Sigfus's painting ended up there as well, muses Hanna, jotting down the gallery's name. It would be interesting to find a painting by Sigfus Gunnarsson, unknown in Iceland until now, somewhere on the Jutland countryside in Denmark.

Hanna keeps on looking but does not find anything further about the butcher, and as she walks downtown to her lunch date, she is still no nearer the truth about *The Birches*. Mr. Jensen at the auction house hasn't gotten back in touch, which is no more than she expected.

She feels she is just not getting anywhere. The joint exhibition venture has also come to a halt. Haraldur is not answering his phone, neither Leifur nor Anselma can give her a clear idea of what they are going to display, and Jon has gone back home to Antwerp. The article Hanna intended to write for the booklet is not coming together either; it is as if everything is frozen over, just like nature. After a mild and rainy January, winter has set in with snow and frost. Not beautiful, still winter days as in Holland; here there's been low pressure, gales, whirling snowstorms, and drifting snow all around.

Hanna is late getting to the restaurant, but she is still the first one there. She smiles to herself, glad to be back home, where it is quite natural to be a bit unpunctual. The restaurant only serves healthy vegetarian dishes, and she reads the menu with mistrust. Having lived with Frederico for years, her taste in food has become rather Italian, and she is not keen on super-healthy food. In the end she orders vegetable lasagna just as Gudny arrives at the table, and she orders the same without asking what it is. She is out of breath and explains she is late because the road across the moor was in a bad state.

"I took my own car. I'm more at ease in a Jeep out in the country," she says. "Then I parked the car outside the parliament building and got caught up in a snowstorm walking across here!" She brushes the snow from her blonde highlights; any hairstyle she may have had has now been blown away.

"But it was fun over at the prison," she says, laughing. "An amazing woman has taken over there." Gudny is referring to the new prison chief who has revamped operations. "She's really giving these men an opportunity," she says. "We were also talking about the young ones; a case came up the other day about a youngster who wanted to go to prison rather than to a young offenders' institution out in the countryside."

Smiling, covered in snow, and rosy-cheeked, she shakes her head in surprise. Hanna looks at her fondly, at her big smile. Hearing her familiar, lively laughter, Hanna is pleased to see her friend again, and her concerns about *The Birches* and the disagreement between the artists pale in significance compared to all that Gudny has to deal with in her job as minister of justice. Gudny makes light of it and praises her colleagues. The signs of weariness are not lost on Hanna, but she sees that Gudny is enjoying her work and she's glad for her. Gudny always wanted to go far.

By the time Laufey arrives, they have already begun eating, and, again, Hanna feels how important their friendship is to her. She does not have much contact with her family now that her parents have died; she never was close to her half brothers and sisters. It is her friends who are her link between the past and the present, between her life before she moved abroad and her life now. They have known one another for about twenty years, some of them for longer. The bonds of friendship have not broken even though they seldom meet.

"They've both grown taller than me," Laufey is saying proudly of her two sons. She is sitting in a thick padded anorak with an African band wrapped around her head as always, and she seems untouched by age. They talk about their children; Gudny answers her phone. It's hectic in the restaurant; people are coming and going and they each keep glancing up at the clock. There is more stress here than in Amsterdam, despite the lack of punctuality. Gudny is talking to someone on the phone about a group of youngsters who were arrested downtown in a derelict house recently. Hanna hears what she is saying without eavesdropping, but when Gudny mentions graffiti, Hanna is all ears. When Gudny hangs up, Hanna tells her how some of the city's outdoor artworks have been vandalized.

"I think I know which kids we're talking about, Hanna," replies Gudny with her mouth full. The phone rings again, but she turns it to silent and slips it into her bag. "Now I can eat in peace for a moment," she says with a broad grin.

"Do you really think it's them?" asks Hanna, surprised. "The ones you were talking about, who were arrested?"

Gudny swallows and nods. "Exactly. They're a small gang, maybe four to six kids, one is only thirteen. They've been graffitiing on walls in derelict buildings in town, both inside and out. There's very little we can do about it. The police take them down to the station, either call the child social work team or their parents, take a statement from them, and then their parents fetch them or the police drive them home. I think the thirteen-year-old is on the child protection register, probably has an impossible home situation, the poor thing."

"Isn't it possible to do something for these kids? Give them some walls to spray as they please or something?" Hanna asks, but Gudny shakes her head.

"We've tried all that long ago. It makes no difference—problem kids just aren't interested. That is, part of this graffiti culture is the excitement of doing something forbidden. Although they do sometimes get punished, for example, one lad was made to clean up the wall of a house he'd spray-painted."

"I see," says Hanna. "Art students from the Academy paint on walls where it's permitted. They know what they're about, and they want to do something stunning."

"Mmm," replies Gudny, looking at the clock. Hanna does not mind.

"I feel sorry for these kids," Hanna says. "I had it so good when I was a child. It would never have occurred to me to go and graffiti a wall."

Laufey laughs. "I don't suppose there was a lot of that in Leirhofn or Kopasker?" Hanna smiles back, recalling the little village in the north of the country where she was born and brought up.

"I was always happy at home in Leirhofn." She stares pensively out of the window, at the drifting snow. "I remember my bedroom window so well. It faced out toward the mountains, and when I sat up in bed I could see right up their slopes. I never wanted to have curtains. The hillsides, the snow, and the crags were like a graphics painting in wintertime. And in the summers I looked right onto the hollows full of berries. And in the evenings..." Falling silent for a moment, Hanna slips back in time and pictures the rural area she was brought up in. "In the evenings the slopes were a reddish-pink. Those mountains were like a friendly giant's embrace."

"Weren't you only a young girl when you moved?" Gudny has finished eating and signals to the waiter. Hanna notices that she gets immediate service. She also notices that people at nearby tables recognize who Gudny is, but no one has bothered them.

"The earthquake was in '76. I was nine then."

"Where were you when it happened?" asks Laufey. Hanna has never talked about that time, and she hesitates. She is not sure she wants to go over that day. She was about to mentally raise her sword in self-defense, look up at the clock, and mention something about time flying, but she changes her mind. Why should she not tell them what happened? It was so long ago. She still glances at the clock, as a precaution, so she can stop when she wants, make the time an excuse to go.

"I was in school." She hesitates, the earthquake vivid before her even though it was over thirty years ago. "The walls and the floor were like waves. It was as if a blow thundered down on the building. Books tumbled off their shelves. Somehow we all got out and no one was hurt."

Hanna takes a sip of water. Gudny stops, her phone halfway out of her bag.

"Then they drove us home," Hanna goes on. "You see, the school was in Kopasker and children from the surrounding farms were bused in. There were crevices in the road, deep fissures created by the earthquake." Hanna does not mention the fear that reigned in the school bus, the silence; no one knew what things would be like at home, what awaited them.

"When I came home, I was so lucky—I immediately saw Mom in the doorway. None of our family was injured." Hanna hesitates again; she feels that no words can express what happened that day. She has always thought that it was then that her parents decided to split up. But in fact it was not like that. The family moved to Akureyri; the divorce came later. But she cannot help herself. She has always thought that if the earthquake had not destroyed their house, if they had not had to move, then her life would have been different and better. But she does not say any of this.

"There was rice pudding all over the kitchen floor," she says lightheartedly instead. "Rice pudding, raisins, and broken crockery. And the fridge and cooker that stood up against opposite walls had met in the middle of the room." She smiles at Laufey. Gudny picks up her phone and checks her missed calls.

"Gudny," says Hanna suddenly, without thinking, maybe because she wants to change the subject. "I would like to do something for these kids who are in trouble. Or for that young lad—is it possible to help him in some way? Perhaps the gallery can do something, or the Annexe, possibly some project for youngsters? Make our town beautiful or something along those lines?" Hanna cannot stop thinking about this lad, the youngest member of the group. What sort of a life must he have if he is considered a case for the child protection register? Maybe his family split up like hers did and he doesn't have a mother to give him the love and security that she enjoyed.

"I'll look into it, Hanna," says Gudny, smiling at her. Hanna senses that Gudny finds her overly sentimental, but she doesn't care. She doesn't have to keep a professional distance when faced with the difficult lives of these youngsters. In her head she immediately starts on a letter to the mayor. The gallery needs extra funds this year because the cost of cleaning up the vandalism has run over budget. Working with the youth could be part of that package. She can see herself organizing something with Agusta, even though it would only be a Saturday afternoon, one weekend.

Hanna is deep in thought when Gudny gets up to go. She hugs them good-bye while talking on the phone, and is still talking as she pays the bill and disappears. Her driver is waiting.

Laufey appears in no hurry, and Hanna is quick to suggest a slice of chocolate cake for dessert. She needs to talk to her and preferably in private. This is an ideal opportunity, and she has been thinking all morning how to approach the subject of Steinn.

He has been off sick. "Steinn, who is never ill," said Edda over the coffee machine that morning. "I've worked with Steinn for seven years and he's never had a single sick day."

Hanna had immediately suspected what was wrong but said nothing. The previous week she had looked up glaucoma on the

Internet and read about the symptoms of slow onset glaucoma. These could well explain Steinn's behavior. A person's peripheral vision deteriorates slowly but surely, creating blind spots, but the central vision remains largely untouched. If nothing is done about it, the condition will progress and cause blindness; people frequently do not notice the deterioration until it is too late. Acute glaucoma, on the other hand, can cause blindness in a very short space of time, in a matter of hours if nothing is done. Hanna does not know if slow onset glaucoma can change into acute or what is really the matter with Steinn, who is never ill. She doesn't really feel she can call him; she can't think up a good reason that doesn't sound odd. Questioning him about his health seems almost like a vote of no confidence, and it would be inappropriate to keep asking him about it. She has decided to be patient, and besides she knows that Steinn doesn't care for help or sympathy; he is a very proud man. She hopes that someone else, someone close to him, will see to it that he gets the help he needs, but she is not so sure.

The slices of cake arrive at the table immediately. Hanna and Laufey are probably getting the benefit of Gudny's ministerial status, even though she has left. Hanna needs to get straight to the point because neither of them has much time. She tells Laufey what she thinks Steinn is suffering from and asks for her professional opinion as a doctor, what she should do. Laufey gives her a curious look.

"So you're taking quite an interest in this man?"

Hanna does not deny it. She decides to be frank. "I'm not exactly falling for him, but there's something about him, Laufey. I don't quite know. Anyway, there's nothing between us. Besides, he's married."

"And so are you," says Laufey, smiling. Hanna smiles back.

"Whether I like Steinn is not the point. I'm just concerned about him."

"How is Frederico anyway?" Laufey interrupts. "How is the long-distance relationship going?"

Hanna sighs silently. Laufey always senses what is on Hanna's mind. She can't get away from it.

"Things aren't entirely OK between us," she says, setting her fork and a delicious bit of cake back down on the plate. Then she comes out with it. Says it out loud for the first time since she stumbled on what was going on; she feels as if she is looking down into an abyss. "He's been seeing someone else."

The words sound banal and ordinary. She does not look at Laufey as she says it, not into her warm dark eyes, but past her, at the people at the next table, a young couple who are eating soup. They look as if they are in love. She looks at the girl; she seems so young, too young to have a boyfriend. She looks past them and out onto the street, looks at the scene through Frederico's eyes, as he saw it, that winter when he tried to live here. It is cold, gray, and ugly. She feels so downcast.

Laufey must see it, too, because she lays her hand on Hanna's arm. They sit in silence for a while. Laufey carries on eating. She waits, giving Hanna the opportunity to say something further, but she doesn't.

"Steinn is just a friend," she says instead. "He's been a friend to me ever since I began there." Hanna feels Laufey's eyes on her, senses the doubts she does not put into words, and for a second she is uncertain of herself. Is Steinn really a friend or does he just need a helping hand? She is not entirely sure but leans toward the feeling of friendship. Yes, he is a true friend.

"I don't know how I can put this to him or get him to go to the doctor's. Or how he can get an appointment at the hospital. I think it's too important for him to delay any longer." Hanna forces herself to eat the chocolate cake, and after she has swallowed a few mouthfuls she feels better. She knows that Laufey will not mention Frederico again, and she is grateful to her for that. She won't talk to anyone else about it either, and Hanna is relieved to have a friend she can trust.

"What about his wife?" asks Laufey.

"She is an artist, and they have two children, quite small I think," replies Hanna.

"Do you know her?"

Hanna shakes her head.

"You should just tell him straight-out, Hanna, ask the man about it. Give him a kick," says Laufey. "It can't go on like this. You can point him in the right direction, to the eye clinic at the hospital. I wish I could help more, but I have to go now."

Laufey and Hanna both get up and hug each other and all that is left unsaid between them is expressed in that embrace. For the first time since Hanna realized what was going on, she finds herself holding back her tears. Until now, her anger at her husband has been overwhelming, but Laufey's empathy helps dissolve those feelings. Hanna needs to make up her mind whether she wants to stay in the marriage. She needs to know in her heart whether she is doing it for her own sake or for Heba, and she hasn't yet made that decision.

When Hanna gets back to the gallery, an e-mail from the auction house where Elisabet Valsdottir bought *The Birches* is waiting for her. She is surprised to hear back from Mr. Jensen. The e-mail reveals the name of the first auction house, the one that sold the paintings from the butcher's collection, where *The Birches* was originally bought, but not the name of the middleman. Hanna can see that Steinn is right; this kind of information is not handed out on a plate. She contacts the auction house immediately and quickly receives an e-mail listing all the works the auction house sold from the butcher's collection. Not one of them is attributed to Gudrun Johannsdottir, and the list doesn't include photos of the paintings. It only gives the title, subject matter, size, and artist's name, but in some cases the painter is unknown. There is only one oil painting the same size as *The Birches*. It is dated the first half of the twentieth century. The motif is given as a birch thicket, but no mention of a mountain or of Iceland. The painter is listed as unknown, the value a fraction of the eight million kronur that Elisabet paid for it. Hanna goes through the list carefully. There is only one work that is a possibility. Finally she sends a note of thanks and asks for a photo of painting number thirty-seven, painter unknown.

Something doesn't ring quite true. Why is the landscape just listed as a birch copse when Mount Baula is such a critical element in the painting? And it clearly is not a Danish landscape. Hanna is deep in thought when she hears Steinn's voice out front. So he can't be very ill, which is a relief.

Edda and Steinn are standing in the corridor and Hanna rushes out, eager and happy. She is pleased that there's nothing seriously wrong with Steinn, and she wants to tell him about the e-mail from the auction house. She is even more relieved when she hears him tell Edda that he has been to the doctor and says, "My wife sent me to the optometrist!"

Hanna walks toward Steinn with a smile, hardly noticing the dark-haired woman standing with him and Edda. She assumes the woman is there to see Edda because they are chatting and laughing at something.

"So you're here!" she says. She looks at him happily, but is taken aback when she sees that he is holding the dark-haired woman by the hand. She is tall and slender and very good-looking. Hanna immediately realizes that this must be Steinn's wife. She instinctively adopts the en garde position, winds down her delight at seeing Steinn again, and pulls her face back to neutral, dulling the glow in her eyes.

The two women size each other up. Hanna makes sure she keeps her expression detached and holds out her hand.

"You must be Helga. Steinn has told me about you. I'm Hanna—I'm the director of the Annexe."

Helga smiles wholeheartedly at her, evidently concluding that she has nothing to fear where Hanna is concerned. To be so unexciting is hurtful to Hanna; maybe this is why Frederico was unfaithful?

Helga and Steinn are tall and make a stunning couple. They seem to have a happy, loving relationship, and Hanna feels a flare of bitter envy and jealousy at their happiness.

"Nice to meet you," says Helga. "Steinn speaks highly of you."

Hanna becomes mindful of the fact that she has not mentioned Steinn to Frederico.

"Helga is an artist," says Steinn, and Hanna can hear the pride in his voice.

"I'm familiar with your work," says Hanna, as if she were on the fencing piste about to attack. She falls silent, which speaks volumes about Helga's painting. Touche, she thinks to herself. She is ashamed of her unseemly behavior but cannot help herself. She has been put in the balance and found wanting. The only course in this situation is self-defense.

When Steinn comes into the office a moment later, he is on his own.

"Were you ill?" asks Hanna cautiously, not sure how he might react to her question or whether he picked up on the tension between her and Helga, but Steinn gives no indication if he has.

"No, no," he says calmly. "Helga sent me to the optometrist, and we made an appointment at the hospital. I need an operation. But there's a long wait, a few months." He feels in his shirt pocket and pulls out a little vial of drops. "Until then I have to use these. And I'm not allowed to drive. That's why Helga is here. She's looking after me like a baby."

Hanna nods and doesn't ask any further questions, doesn't even mention the glaucoma.

"I've been in contact with both auction houses," she says. Steinn looks at her quizzically. "I still haven't found out who bought the painting before Elisabet. But I'm waiting for a photo from the first auction house," she adds. "So we can be sure it's the same painting."

"Hmm," says Steinn but nothing more.

Hanna does not know what he is thinking. She hears Edda's footsteps approaching from behind.

"I really ought to show you something, Hanna," says Steinn hurriedly. "Have you got a moment to have a quick look now?"

Hanna agrees straightaway. She also wants to talk about this in private, so she follows Steinn out of the office and down to the basement, where *The Birches* is standing on an easel against a wall. Hanna has come to really dislike this work she once thought was so beautiful.

"You don't think we can actually continue with this, do you?" she asks, partly hoping that Steinn will be in agreement. She is not sure she wants to turn up every possible stone, but she is also ashamed of thinking like that. Not to bother investigating the painting to the fullest would be like taking part in the forgery herself, if indeed it is a forgery.

But Steinn doesn't respond. He clutches his head in his hands and staggers forward. Hanna sees beads of sweat appear on his upper lip; he groans and leans heavily against the table. Hanna reaches out her hand.

"Is everything all right?"

"No, I don't think it is." Steinn sits down on a stool, holding his head. When he looks up, one eye is red and bloodshot.

"I can't see," he says, trying to stand, but he loses his balance and stumbles. Hanna goes to steady him, but he falls to the floor with his hands to his head.

Hanna crouches down next to him, makes sure he is breathing, grabs her cell phone out of her pocket, and calls for an ambulance and then up to Edda. Within seconds Edda and the other women are down in the basement. Hanna tells them not to panic; the ambulance is on its way. Agusta goes back up to watch for it, and Edda calls Helga, who left only a short while ago.

Hanna is scared. She feels her heart thumping in her chest; she feels frightened for Steinn lying there unconscious on the floor. She crouches down next to him and holds his cold, clammy hand. What could it have been that he wanted to show her? He must have gotten the X-ray of the painting. Curious, she looks around but can't see anything. Besides, it's even more cluttered with paintings and various artifacts down here than usual.

It has been a busy week preparing for the opening next weekend. The walls had to be repainted, so the paintings that would otherwise permanently hang in the gallery have been moved. Steinn has removed Sigfus Gunnarsson's painting, *Composition in Blue*, which the gallery was given the year before, down from the wall on the staircase and temporarily made space for it in the basement. It is now standing on the floor, shrouded in Bubble Wrap, in Hanna's line of vision as she crouches down holding Steinn's hand.

She keeps half an eye on Steinn, who is breathing evenly, although he's pale and beads of perspiration glisten on his forehead.

The outlines of the painting are clearer through the plastic. There is a half-moon, divided by a diagonal line. She has seen this line before, this shape, but she can't remember where, she is in such a state. The painting is on its side, and Hanna sees it from a new perspective. But she doesn't think about that; she is thinking about Steinn. She is fond of him; she cannot imagine losing his friendship. He has supported her from her very first day, he has kept an eye on her at work, and he has been there for her whenever she has needed him. She stares at him, then at the painting, back at Steinn, and then finally, after what seems like an eternity, she hears footsteps and the EMTs' voices. She explains what happened, tells them about the headaches, the shooting pain in his eye, and how it went all bloodshot.

"I think he's had an attack of acute glaucoma," says Hanna.

"What makes you say that?" asks an EMT.

Hanna gives a hurried and rather muddled response because there's no time to lose and she doesn't think they are really listening. "Just look in his shirt pocket—he's got eye drops. He was at the optometrist yesterday."

The man fumbles in his pocket, but there is nothing there; the vial has either fallen out or Steinn has put it down. He looks at Edda and Agusta. "Did you know that he had glaucoma?"

Edda shakes her head and looks at Hanna in surprise. "He was at the optometrist, I know that much. But he never mentioned glaucoma." She looks at Baldur, who has also come down, and he shakes his head. Nobody is aware that Steinn has glaucoma.

Having lifted Steinn onto the stretcher, the EMTs now stand up, every movement quick and well practiced. Hanna and the others shrink to one side and watch them carry the stretcher up the stairs.

"Just call the hospital," one of the men says to Hanna as they disappear up the steps. Hanna would really have liked to go with them, but she doesn't. She is only a work colleague, and naturally Helga will be going up there straightaway. But supposing Steinn hasn't mentioned to her about the glaucoma? Hanna is not sure that he has. Glaucoma is a serious condition, and Steinn is not likely to want to give Helga cause for concern.

When the EMTs have gone, they are all left standing there worried. Edda goes to make coffee, her automatic response to any difficulty. Hanna is concerned that she may be the only one who knows that Steinn might have glaucoma. She doesn't want to call Helga. That would be odd. And maybe Helga saw how she looked at Steinn. She isn't even sure herself how she looked at him. But it's vital that the hospital staff give him the right treatment.

Hanna hesitates briefly then goes out into the reception area, where no one can hear her, calls the hospital, and asks for Laufey. She is busy. Hanna tells the receptionist that this is an emergency. She is advised to call the emergency room and give them the relevant information. Hanna calls and the receptionist there says she will pass her message on. Hanna tells her that Steinn could go blind if he doesn't get the right treatment straightaway. The receptionist agrees and repeats that she will ensure the information gets to the right person. Hanna hangs up, worried that this won't be enough. She fears that Steinn might lose his sight because of a doctor's mistake. She tries to get through to Laufey again but fails. She calls her cell, but Laufey doesn't pick up. Eventually she gives up calling. Mentally she moves into the neutral position to calm her mind before setting off for the hospital.

Hanna fears bumping into Helga in the emergency room, but she has already gone in with Steinn. Hanna learns that he is merely under investigation. An optometrist has not been sent for. Hanna goes out again and into the main entrance to look for Laufey. She must get a hold of someone in the hospital who will listen to her. Eventually she finds the physical rehabilitation department, where Laufey is doctor-in-charge.

Hanna enters the corridor, glances around, peeps into the ward, and sees Laufey talking to a patient in one of the rooms. Hanna waits outside, and when Laufey walks back out, she is startled to see Hanna there, out of breath and looking uneasy. Hanna briefly tells her the whole story, and Laufey takes her by the hand, leads her into the visitors' room, and tells her to take a seat and wait. Then she goes back into the department, leaving Hanna there on her own.

She sits restlessly and sees again and again the image of Steinn putting his hand up to his right eye, red and bloodshot. She sees the painting against the wall, *Composition in Blue*. She can picture it, the half-moon, cut through with straight lines, the interplay of blue and yellow colors, and at last it occurs to her where she has seen these lines before.

It was when she and Steinn were looking at images of *The Birches* on the computer. When Steinn showed her the infrared image. The drawing underneath the painting, curved lines cut through with straight lines. She'd thought maybe they were a bridge or a boat. But now she is absolutely certain. They are the same shapes. There can be no doubt about it.

Hanna has a photographic memory. Her memories are stored as pictures; her brain is a database of hundreds of paintings that she can recall whenever, their colors, light, shapes, and lines. She is never mistaken.

Underneath *The Birches* lies a drawing that is based on similar lines and shapes as *Composition in Blue* by Sigfus Gunnarsson. For whatever reason. She does not try to understand it now; her mind is too taken up with Steinn.

Laufey comes back in after a while. "He's going for tests in the ophthalmology unit. He is on his way there now." She smiles encouragingly at Hanna. "It'll be all right. He'll get all the help available. It was just as well this thing about his acute glaucoma came out. His wife is with him," she adds with a mischievous look. Hanna pretends not to hear the tone in her voice or see the amusement in her eye and just thanks her for her help.

Laufey goes back to work, but Hanna remains on the sofa in the visitors' room for a moment. She thinks about paintings. About the ones she is most fond of and goes back to again and again. She pictures the wide expanse of the sky in Jacob van Ruisdael's paintings, the tranquil landscape paintings of Camille Corot, the soft light in paintings by Claude Lorainn, and the pinkish-red hues of the mountainsides from home. She thinks about Heba.

6

ARTIST IN THE MAKING

Kari has his dad's brown eyes; he has just turned thirteen and looks like an angel. Dark hair, fashionably long, and girlish good-looks. His eyes are furtive and also innocent, giving him the air of a defenseless animal. Looking at him you cannot avoid feeling some sort of sympathy, a desire to give him a helping hand, to do something for him. His sisters are different. Saerun, the younger one, is a tough cookie and cheeky with it, and she uses foul language comically at odds with her five years. At fifteen, Soffia is the eldest. She looks after them and is just waiting for tenth grade to finish so she can start working. None of them has the same father; this home has never known a dad.

They live in a two-room basement flat on Njalsgata, just behind Snorrabraut. Their mom sleeps in the living room when she is home, the sisters share the lower bunk in the bedroom, and Kari has the top bunk. They have a desk in the bedroom, no wardrobe, and their clothes lie in scattered heaps on the floor.

The children fend for themselves, and their mother is proud of the way they manage. There is no way of knowing whether there will be food in the house, and they never have a packed lunch for school. The social workers have paid them more than one visit, and up until now they have deemed it better for the children to stay together than be put in foster care with separate families. Then there are long periods when things run smoothly, more or less. Now is not one of those times, and Kari wakes feeling tired. He has a headache and his tummy aches; he is late for school, and Soffia and Saerun have already left.

He gets up and goes through to the kitchen. There are dirty dishes and glasses, empty yogurt cups, and a liter of milk in the fridge that has gone sour. He has a drink of water, searches for his clothes and his backpack in the bedroom, then gives up halfway through—he sees no point in turning up late for school only to be told off and he is too tired anyway. He was out with his crew the night before. The oldest boys are already seventeen and eighteen, and they often have cigarettes and even share a joint, sometimes a beer. They were doing a piece on an inside wall in Hverfisgata and they gave him free rein—him, the youngest. He is proud because in the end he did the wall almost all by himself, in his own style. The others haven't quite got what it takes, the right touch. He decides to go and look at the wall again. If he could just get a hold of a cell phone somewhere he could take a picture. Maybe he will find a phone in a cafe. People are often so careless with their phones; they leave them lying on the table and don't notice when they disappear.

Kari puts on the same jeans he wore yesterday and the week before and a black hoodie. Neither is clean, but he's not concerned. He glances out of the window. It's not raining so he doesn't bother with his coat, which he cannot stand—he would rather be cold than walk around in that crummy garment.

He pulls his cap down to his eyes and goes out, slamming the door behind him. He doesn't bother locking it—there's nothing worth taking anyway.

He starts at Subway, but the man behind the cash register kicks him straight out again. He knows Kari and he knows that he does not have any money, but he hands him a buttered roll as he shows him the door. Chewing on the bread, Kari tries another cafe around the corner. He walks around slowly as though looking for someone, as though expecting someone. The girl behind the counter looks at him with suspicion in her eyes—a youngster in town during school hours is suspicious.

Kari moves out of her line of sight. He finds his victim toward the back of the room near the toilets. A middle-aged man is sitting down reading the papers, and his cell phone is lying on the table. Kari steals a look around. There are not many people in the cafe; it doesn't look as if anyone will ruin his plans, no one at the counter that he needs to run past, no one at the entrance. Quick as a flash he grabs the phone and makes a run for it, out, over the street, and across the square by the art gallery, where he is far too visible. From there he shoots down a side alley, behind the Thai restaurant, where he crouches down behind the garbage cans, waiting.

He is sweating and out of breath. He doesn't feel good; his heart is thumping. It's been a while since he has eaten properly. Soffia doesn't know how to cook and often buys sweets for Saerun to keep her happy rather than buying a meal. Soffia looks after Saerun as best she can—as well as any child can look after another child, when she doesn't know what it is to be looked after herself. She doesn't know how to, doesn't think about cleanliness or healthy food or sleeping patterns, but she gives Saerun hugs and lets her fall asleep in her lap. Soffia can't leave, Kari thinks to himself. Much as they fight, he cannot even begin to think about it. He couldn't look after Saerun. He doesn't even know if he likes her. Most of the time he finds her a pain.

Kari does not dwell on these thoughts. What matters to him most is his crew, graffitiing—he feels good when he is bombing, which is all too rarely. He can't afford cannons. He cannot hear anyone chasing him and opens his clammy fist to examine the phone; yesss, it's got a camera and the battery is charged. Shoving the phone into his pocket he heads up a side street rather than the main shopping street, because there are fewer people around. He feels like everyone is looking at him, a boy who isn't at school; he wants to be left in peace. He doesn't care that he's skipped classes; he's done it often and there have been no repercussions. They threaten to expel him, tell him off, but none of that bothers him because these people don't matter to him. I don't matter to them either, he thinks to himself.

At last he reaches the derelict house where he and his friends spent the previous evening. He crawls in through a broken basement window and holds his breath against the smell of excrement and urine. In the half dark he fumbles his way toward the stairs up to the ground floor and then on up a wooden staircase to the second floor once he has made sure there is no one around. He is frightened of bumping into one of the old winos or crazed drug addicts who crash out there, but luck is on his side—the building is empty. He goes straight into a large room on the second floor, gets the cell phone out, and photographs the wall. This will go straight onto the Internet; he is proud of this wall. The whole expanse is awash in color, covered uncontrollably in white, gray, and violet, shadows of something he feels inside but does not know exactly what, something that draws him back again and again and allows him to forget.

The moment he has finished taking his photos, he hears men's loud voices and noisy footsteps on the stairs. It's the police! He is about to shove the phone in his pocket when one of the police officers whips it from him and holds Kari in a firm but gentle grip. Kari doesn't answer their questions. They mean nothing to him; they cannot touch him—all they can do is take a statement from him down at the police station and drive him home.

This is the second time that he has been arrested recently. The duty sergeant recognizes him. He is friendly, asks Kari if he's hungry or cold. But Kari doesn't fall for these friendly overtures; he just shakes his head and gives the policemen monosyllabic answers. Virtually the whole group was arrested last time; they were all picked up by their parents, except Kari, who was driven home, as he is again this time.

He is sullen and angry at himself for being caught, and when he sees his mother sleeping in the living room, his feelings overwhelm him. It is more peaceful when she is not home. She wakes up when the policemen come in, and Kari sees her turn on the charm, making out that she is just fine while she talks to them. She claims to be surprised; she doesn't understand this at all—it must be a new phase that will pass. Kari's mom is still young, and despite her dissolute life she is still beautiful. Kari can tell she's been drinking, but probably not since the previous evening; she isn't drunk. He waits till the policemen have left before asking her for money.

7

EXHIBITION OPENING
COPENHAGEN, SPRING 2005

The opening of the fine arts exhibition is being held at the Icelandic–Danish Cultural Association in the newly renovated docklands area, and the building is bursting at the seams. Crowds of people are standing or sitting at tables on the white paving stones in front of the glass building on a sunny afternoon in May. The sun reflects off the water and mirrors through the glass; the white pavement intensifies the brightness.

Inside is a plentiful supply of food. Trays piled with national gourmet cuisine with a modern twist glide around on the arms of courteous waiters: minute blood sausage tartlets, salted meat in aspic served in little aluminum dishes, croutons of rye bread with lamb pate on sticks. A band is due to start shortly, to appeal to the young people who perhaps don't have an awful lot of interest in Icelandic painters who studied in Copenhagen in the middle of the last century. There are paintings by Thorarin B. Thorlaksson, Kristin Jonsdottir, Sigfus Gunnarsson, Thorvald Skulason, and Gudrun Johannsdottir among others. All paintings are from the earlier parts of their careers, landscape, a touch of cubism, a hint of romanticism, and some expressionism. Still life paintings, scenes through a window, harbor views, street scenes, and landscapes. Sigfus was one of the most ambitious. Both his sketchbooks and his cubist face paintings are on display, and his semiabstract paintings stand out with their vivid colors.

Standing with an exhibition program in one hand and a soda water in the other, Hrafn Arnason looks around the room. Hrafn is a regular visitor to Copenhagen because the company has its factories here. In previous years the company produced frozen prawns and smoked salmon, but now it produces fresh sushi and sashimi, which it sells in gourmet delicatessens in Denmark and Sweden. Business is going well; sushi bars are trendy. Hrafn is hoping to meet an acquaintance here who has recently bought up a hotel. The idea is to get him to open a sushi bar inside and Hrafn will offer him a discount on his products. Hrafn is always on the lookout for new business opportunities; he wants to expand, and he needs more regular customers. He likes best to see to everything himself—just like his father before him. He knows most of his staff and prefers to employ Icelanders, even here in Copenhagen, and he regularly visits the site at Norrebro where the packing is done and watches the work being carried out.

Hrafn is standing so stock-still he is nearly invisible, alone with his thoughts in the crowd. Someone suddenly attracts his attention, fair hair, brown eyes, a slender body; then Masha's face fills his line of vision and she kisses him three times. Hrafn hasn't seen Masha and Larisa since the previous year, at the business conference in Moscow. As soon as he sees Masha, he wonders how many restaurants she owns in Moscow. Until now he has stuck to Copenhagen and Malmo in Sweden, but there is no reason why he shouldn't sell sushi to Moscow. He catches Larisa's eye. He has not forgotten her, despite his efforts to, and he slides his hands up into his sleeves, feeling embarrassed.

"Call me Masha, Mr. Arnason. How lovely to see you again!" Mariya says loudly. Her English is as stiff as before, and she lets her Russian accent show through. Mariya is a powerful woman from a powerful country; she does not need to submit to other nations' rules of pronunciation.

"I didn't know there were artists in Iceland," continues Masha with a smile. "Larisa told me there were only a handful." Larisa smiles politely at Hrafn, her eyes constantly wandering to the paintings on the walls. She clearly has more interest in them than in Hrafn, and he is relieved and disappointed at the same time. He follows her gaze, and, because he does not know what they want of him, to break the ice he begins talking about Icelandic art.

When he talks about the first Icelandic painters, their innovative work, how they had to go abroad to study, and how most of them came to Copenhagen, Larisa is all ears, which surprises him. She looks intently at the paintings as Hrafn explains how they went all out in the fight for independence at the turn of the century and painted the beauty of the Icelandic countryside, rural prosperity, and bright, clear nights. He also mentions their value and supply and demand and talks about the careers of Sigfus Gunnarsson and Svavar Gudnasonar, who were both connected to the CoBrA movement. "The works of Sigfus and Svavar are amongst those that fetch the highest prices," he says and mentions a sum. He is careful what he says because he is not an expert like Larisa and he doesn't care to reveal his lack of knowledge.

"I bought a painting not long ago that could be by this woman," he says a moment later, pointing to a painting by Gudrun Johannsdottir. Masha nods, taking in what he says, but her mind is clearly elsewhere. Larisa has moved to the other side of the room, where she is looking at Sigfus Gunnarsson's sketchbooks in a display cabinet.

By chance, the director of the cultural association suddenly appears and greets Hrafn with open arms; she used to know his parents. Hrafn introduces her to Masha, not quite knowing what to say.

"We met at a business conference in Moscow last year," he says finally.

The director introduces Hrafn to a woman standing at her side. "This is Hanna Jonsdottir; she's an art historian. She wrote a piece in the exhibition program for us and helped us with Gudrun's paintings."

Courteously, Hrafn offers her a firm handshake, briefly taking in her delicate features and gray eyes, her smooth brown hair drawn back in a ponytail. Mousy, he thinks, glancing quickly at her dark gray cotton dress.

Not unattractive for an entrepreneur, thinks Hanna. From the corner of her eye she notices how he draws his hands up into his sleeves so they are less conspicuous. She smiles politely.

"Hrafn has a good collection of paintings," the director is saying to Hanna.

"Perhaps you have something by Gudrun? They're still searching for paintings by her," Hanna asks, but Hrafn shakes his head. Excusing himself, he turns back to Masha and casts his eye around for Larisa. He still does not know what these Russian women want of him and that bothers him. He wants to get to the bottom of it; he wants to have things under control.

A camera flashes on the other side of the room, and Hrafn thinks he sees Larisa slipping her camera back into her bag; she is standing by the cabinet where Sigfus Gunnarsson's sketchbooks are displayed. She walks toward him smiling. Her eyes are no longer scanning the paintings; instead they rest a good while on Hrafn. He suddenly feels very warm, but just then he spots the acquaintance he was looking for. The hotel owner. And prospective sushi bar owner, though he doesn't know it yet. Let off the hook, Hrafn greets him with delight. He is not sure he could resist Larisa's beauty again. Hrafn introduces his colleague to Masha, and she greets him with great interest. Is this what she's after, he wonders as he introduces them and sees the mutual business interest in their eyes, a mixture of curiosity, greed, and cunning. They briefly exchange courtesies and then Masha suddenly excuses herself. Larisa follows her like a shadow. They are some paces away when Masha turns around.

"Send me a photo of the painting."

Hrafn is surprised at this request. So she did hear what he said about the painting that might be by Gudrun. But he agrees—why not indeed? They are both collectors, though Masha is on a totally different scale than him. Hrafn wants to sell sushi to Moscow and therefore needs Masha's friendship. He is relieved to see Larisa go; the day is too hot and her skin too silky smooth to bear. He pushes away all thoughts of her body and, with business in mind, turns to his colleague.

8

GOLDSMITH FROM BRUGES
REYKJAVIK, CURRENT DAY

Kristin, the gallery director, seems to love staff meetings. "Just so we're all singing from the same song sheet," she says when she calls Baldur asking him to call another meeting. Items on the agenda can be wide-ranging. They need to resolve issues around the coat check, the cafe is not up to scratch, and they need to buy new chairs for the events room. And, of course, they regularly need to discuss exhibits and other things that are going on in the gallery.

In the beginning, these meetings irritated Hanna. She did not appreciate getting a phone call and being required to attend a meeting with half an hour's notice. In the Netherlands she grew accustomed to being organized, but that does not necessarily work well here. On Fridays, before the day is out, she likes to plan the week ahead, but she has often seen her plans fall by the wayside and finds she has to take the week as it comes. They are now sitting in the meeting room choosing among three styles of IKEA coffee mugs for the cafeteria; the cafe manager wants their opinions.

Steinn is still in the hospital; he has been off work for over a week. Hanna sorely misses him; she sees now how much he has helped her. She wants to get back to her work as quickly as possible and, without further ado, points at the mug she likes best. Edda chooses the same one, Agusta goes for the bigger one, and Baldur wants the third option.

"The majority rules," says Kristin with a smile, handing Edda the sheet of paper. "We'll order this one with the saucer and the matching side plate."

Hanna continues to compose the letter in her head, her first letter to the new mayor about the extra work involved to get back on track with the outdoor artworks in need of repair, and also about possible funding for a weekend workshop for youngsters. The vandalism seems to be on the rise, if anything. The statue she and Steinn went to examine is not the only one that has suffered. Steinn had written a report and had begun to clean the statue before he ended up in the hospital, but already there are more repair jobs waiting.

Hanna is also impatiently waiting to hear from Steinn about his discovery; they need to examine the infrared image of *The Birches* painting again, with *Composition in Blue* for comparison. She has not gotten any further in her investigations. Steinn has all the information about *Composition in Blue* and its ownership history, and Hanna cannot work out how a painting that matches it could be hidden under *The Birches* painting. Gudrun would not have painted over a work by Sigfus Gunnarsson, that's for sure. Hanna's thoughts buzz around in circles when she tries to get a grip on it. She heard from Edda that Steinn is doing well and should be coming back to work soon, but she hasn't talked to him herself. Their friendship is not that close; they only know each other through work and have no connection outside of that. It wouldn't be appropriate to trouble him with work matters in the hospital, and she is even less inclined to call him at home and maybe get Helga on the line.

She listens absentmindedly to Kristin talk about the cafeteria and drags her thoughts back to her work, to the unfinished letter on her computer. She suspects there will be more such letters. The mayor will soon discover that Hanna is an expert at this sort of letter writing and it is not worth sidestepping the issues she raises. Years of dealing with bureaucracy in Europe, funding applications, and raising money have made Hanna almost unbeatable when it comes to this sort of thing. Letters like this one are her forte; she manages to appeal to the reader's pretension, patriotism, pride, and professional conscience in such an affable manner that her request is almost always well received. If this doesn't happen the first time around, she writes more letters, and then even more. She gets her way in the end. The new mayor is an art lover, and, besides, it is impossible to refuse necessary maintenance to artworks owned by the city—that would not sit well with public opinion. Hanna can just imagine the headlines in the papers: "New Mayor Leaves *The Water-Bearer* to the Vandals." The locals know their city's statues; they are landmarks that many have known since childhood.

Edda passes a carrot cake around. Hanna smiles at her. Sugar is exactly what is needed to make this meeting bearable, and she helps herself to a generous slice before handing it to Agusta. Baldur and Kristin are discussing something in undertones. Baldur fishes some papers out of a plastic folder, but Hanna barely pays attention. She is just finishing her cake and assumes that the meeting is over. She has the next sentence of the letter formed in her head and then Kristin announces another item on the agenda.

"Do you mean the exhibition with the Austrian twins?" Hanna asks, but Kristin shakes her head.

"No, no, no, that's all sorted. I want to talk about another exhibition. Admittedly it's only in the early stages, and I really want you all to keep up to speed from the beginning because it's very short notice. Baldur has been working on this for the last few weeks and now it's all falling into place." Kristin takes a bite of cake. "Baldur, you tell them about it," she adds with a smug look.

Baldur runs his fingers through his thick hair as if he doesn't know how to begin and puts the papers down on the table. Hanna notices the letterhead is from a well-known gallery in Cologne. The letter is in German and addressed to Baldur personally.

"Well, I've been working on this for a few weeks now," says Baldur, looking at Agusta and Edda but not Hanna.

"Liaising with a German curator who approached me with an idea." He clears his throat. "You know how the Germans are thrilled with Icelandic landscape painting, Icelandic romanticism, and so forth. Well, it's Herbert Grunewald who wants to put on an exhibition with Icelandic and German artists, a large exhibition that will also travel to Cologne and be shown in his gallery there, and maybe in other places, possibly London. Our plan is to put together romantic and contemporary landscape painting, and even those from earlier periods. Herbert could potentially get a hold of paintings by big names that have never been shown here, even classics like Caspar David Friedrich."

Baldur pauses for a moment to let this news have the intended effect. He is talking about one of the most famous romantic painters. That such a small gallery as theirs, in the back of beyond, should have one of his paintings on loan is virtually unheard of in the art world. It would smash all their box office records to date.

Hanna gives him a look of questioning disbelief, and he adds, "Well, maybe not his best-known works, but probably oil paintings nonetheless. This will obviously be the biggest exhibition of the year, and Kristin and I have already begun to sound out Icelandic artists. Ruri, Georg Gudni, Eggert Petursson, and Ragna Robertsdottir will all be included and maybe some others too. The idea is to follow this with a stylish book and have articles about landscape painting in it. The opening will coincide with the Arts Festival this spring."

Hanna does not utter a word but stares dumbfounded at Baldur, who avoids her gaze and begins to hand out copies of the letter from Herbert Grunewald in which he talks about the exhibition and possibly loaning them paintings.

"He also mentions watercolors by Durer," Baldur adds. Then he looks at Hanna, with an unflinching look that says: I dare you. Hanna stares stiffly back at him; she is beside herself with anger. She would love to throw her coffee in his face, and in her head she jumps up onto the table and, drawing her foil from its sheath, aims it at his rib cage, getting the better of him. How dare you, she says silently. How dare you steal my idea!

At one of the first staff meetings after Hanna took over as director of the Annexe she presented her plan in outline and specifically mentioned a landscape exhibition she intended to open in July. She remembers precisely how she worded her plan at the time, and now she repeats the same words again, calmly and questioningly, with a hint of challenge.

"Landscape? Landscape past and present?"

No one utters a word. Kristin munches her cake and doesn't look at her. Agusta turns off her phone and looks down at the table; Edda quickly refills her coffee cup. Agusta too? thinks Hanna. And Edda? Hanna feels that they are all thinking the same thing. They all want Baldur's exhibition at the gallery. It is a much bolder project than the little exhibition Hanna was proposing. Hanna cannot oppose this project either, but right now she is angry first and foremost. She wishes Steinn was at the meeting. She views him as an ally, and it occurs to her that it's undeniably easier for Kristin and Baldur that he is not present as this plan is being put forward. Not that he would have said anything. But Hanna knows what his expression would have been. He would have hidden his thoughts. But there would have been a hint of resentment in his lower lip, which is slightly thicker than the upper one. I alone would have noticed it, she thinks, and that would have spurred me on.

"In fact, I was thinking about your exhibition, Hanna. It will fit in nicely with this project and will back it up," interjects Baldur. "In fact, I was talking about it to Herbert and about the excellent work you're doing here. It is clearly a coincidence that he came to me with precisely the same idea after you outlined yours, but this is on quite a different scale, of course. It must have been something in the air." Baldur smiles warmly.

Hanna looks at Baldur and tries to gauge whether he really stole her idea and presented it to Herbert as his own at some cocktail do and now is attributing the idea to Herbert. Or whether Herbert Grunewald genuinely did have this kind of exhibition in mind and wanted to link it to Icelandic landscape painting. Hanna feels that the phrase *in fact* cropped up too often in Baldur's account for it to be believable. Of course, there is nothing original in putting on an exhibition of landscape paintings. Hanna does not have a patent on such an idea. Yet what Baldur is presenting is precisely the same as what she presented at the meeting some weeks earlier. An interplay of past and present that expresses how landscape has been portrayed in fine art through the ages.

But Hanna also knows that Herbert Grunewald is fascinated by the Icelandic countryside and comes regularly for the salmon fishing; he even owns a cottage in a small village on the eastern fjords. She is well aware who Herbert Grunewald is. He is the director of an exhibition gallery in Cologne. Both he and the gallery are well respected in the international art world. Hanna has frequently viewed exhibitions there. Grunewald was also the previous director of the national gallery in Berlin; the exhibition gallery in Cologne is his passion. He enjoys the benefit of twenty years' worth of connections and has acquired trust from gallery directors and curators throughout Europe and in the States, not forgetting private collectors. He is a big name to say the least.

It would be a wonderful opportunity for Icelandic artists to be able to show their work at an exhibition that has his name attached, let alone exhibit in his gallery in Cologne. It would give their careers a boost and would also draw attention to Icelandic artists who are internationally recognized. Herbert is also a collector; Hanna has even viewed his private collection in

Berlin, which is open to the public one day a month. She made a special trip from Amsterdam to view his collection, etchings and prints of northern European landscapes from the fifteenth to the seventeenth century. She spent a whole day there and would gladly have stayed longer. Hanna doesn't know Herbert personally and has never had dealings with him. Why would he even consider loaning a priceless painting to a small gallery in Reykjavik? His love of Iceland must be exceptional.

Friedrich or Durer, she thinks. That would pull the crowds. And she feels even angrier at not being included in the discussions, being kept out of the loop.

Baldur says nothing further about the uncanny similarities between this exhibition and Hanna's idea, and suddenly she is convinced that this is his doing. Totally contrary to what she expected when she arrived, their acquaintance from art college days hasn't given rise to any significant interaction between them. She sees little of Baldur outside of the staff meetings. He is always friendly, says *Hanna dear* and *my old friend*, but she feels there is nothing to back it up. Baldur would stab her in the back; she doesn't trust him.

But then again? Hanna looks at Agusta. Don't suppose she knows Herbert Grunewald. Hanna vaguely remembers Agusta, who is part of the international gallery directors' group, mentioning that their last joint project took place in the eastern fjords two or three years ago. Maybe they had the use of his house there? Agusta is smart enough to go behind their backs. To get Herbert to contact Baldur, well aware that she would be an important cog in the wheel that drives the exhibition forward. Of course, Agusta doesn't want to lose her good working relationship with Hanna, which could be her reason for operating behind closed doors.

And as the director, Kristin is undoubtedly a friend of Herbert's; she knows everyone in the art world. She is a snob and obviously wants to promote the gallery above all else. Kristin is no friend of Hanna's, although they work together well enough. She certainly would not side with Hanna against the others. Steinn is probably the only one who would do that.

She pushes Herbert's letter away. Maybe one day she will uncover who was behind this, but not today.

"Good luck," she says at last and smiles at Baldur. She sees that he is relieved. He thinks she isn't going to take it any further. But he, or whoever took the idea, has not finished the job, and Hanna is in no mood for laughter. Mentally she lowers her foil, but she doesn't sheath it and remains in the en garde position.

"I will carry on with my plans anyway," she says. "As Baldur said, the two events aren't comparable. My goal is different, and the two should complement one another. I'm just writing an article for the booklet, about landscapes past and present and how the worldview of each age and each nation is revealed in its paintings."

Hanna tries to say this in a light tone—she might even have succeeded. The others don't know that she hasn't started on any such article. She needs to get a move on.

Hanna is almost on her feet when Kristin asks her to wait a moment.

"I want to take this opportunity to let you know that Agusta needs to reduce her hours for the time being. She'll be working half days until the spring."

Hanna looks in surprise at Agusta, who is gathering up her papers and doesn't return her gaze. She doesn't get it. How can Agusta, who is so ambitious, reduce her hours? Hanna looks at her questioningly, but Agusta has her eyes on her papers.

"Agusta will be looking after Kolbeinn, her son, who has been unwell," says Kristin by way of explanation.

Her son? Hanna can't make head or tail of this. Agusta, who lives with her parents. Does she have a child?

"I didn't know you had a child," Hanna exclaims. They have worked together for around two months and Agusta has not mentioned that she has a child. "Why didn't you tell me?" she asks involuntarily.

Agusta looks away, hiding behind the letter from Grunewald, her hands shaking slightly. She lays them down over the letter.

"I would never have asked you to…" Hanna doesn't finish her sentence because Agusta interrupts.

"Exactly. I'm not looking for special treatment because of Kolbeinn. Most people here have children. And Mom has helped out with him. It's not as though I'm alone. You haven't asked me to do anything out of the ordinary."

Hanna falls silent. She has asked Agusta to work late on some occasions, to come in on Saturdays or in the evening when the gallery has been holding an event. She regrets this now.

From the way Agusta put it, Hanna concludes that Kolbeinn's father is not involved in bringing him up. Granny and Grandpa clearly help out. Hanna glances around. No one else is surprised. She is the only one taken off guard at this meeting.

"How old is he?" she asks.

Agusta smiles. "Nearly two." She pulls her wallet out of the bag by her side, eases a little picture out of one compartment, and passes it across the table to Hanna.

"Is he very ill?"

"No, not really. But I'm going to stop sending him to the day care because he's had continuous ear infections since the autumn."

"I wish you'd told me about him earlier," says Hanna. "I have a daughter of my own. She's nearly eighteen. She's with her dad in Amsterdam."

Agusta looks at her in amazement.

"I didn't know that. I thought you were single and had no children."

Hanna can't help laughing, but it touches a nerve as well.

"Why did you think that?"

Agusta is evasive.

"I just assumed it, I suppose. I apologize."

This little polite word, *apologize*, makes Hanna go quiet. She was going to mention the winter when she was alone with Heba after Frederico gave up trying to live in Iceland and left. A year later Hanna moved abroad with Heba to be with him. She wanted her to be with her dad. This formal word stops Hanna from saying anything further. Clearly Agusta wants to maintain her pride; it is very important to her to be professional, and Hanna is not going to deny her that. Besides, they are at a meeting and it wouldn't be appropriate.

Hanna now sees a completely different person than she did a moment ago. Quick as a flash, pieces of the picture reform into a fresh image of Agusta. Gone is the young woman who would rather meet up with her friends on weekends than work, who could not wait to get out of the gallery at four-thirty, who was ambitious yet a touch egocentric. Now Hanna sees the dark rings under her eyes in another light, her rush to get home each day. Her almost undetectable reluctance to work on weekends.

In her place is an ambitious young woman who pours her energy into caring for her son and into her work unstintingly. Nonetheless, Hanna is surprised that Agusta's son has never come up in conversation. Hanna tries to see herself through Agusta's eyes. Why did Agusta think she was single and without a family? Hanna pushes this thought aside. Maybe Frederico was right. Maybe she is cold and unbending.

Hanna catches Kristin's eye looking stiffly at her as if expecting something. Hanna registers what it is she has forgotten.

"Of course you must take off all the time you need, Agusta," she says. "It'll be good for your boy to get rid of these ongoing illnesses." Hanna sees that Agusta is relieved, and they don't discuss it any further. Kristin brings the meeting to a close, reminding them of the next one.

Down in the office Agusta hands Hanna a new report of vandalism to an outdoor artwork.

"Is this a brand-new one?"

Agusta nods. "Yes. Just like the last one, except this is downtown. You can hardly see that statue anymore. I went and took photos the other day because Steinn is ill. Sorry, I just forgot to mention it."

Hanna looks at the report. This time it is a statue of a young girl that has been sprayed over, and she feels a pang of anguish seeing the statue treated in this way.

This is yet another job for Steinn; the gallery's work comes to a grinding halt without him. His position is wide, the investigation into *The Birches* and now probably *Composition in Blue* as well, upkeep of the artworks, and all sorts of maintenance to the building. He is invaluable.

Looking pensively at Steinn's empty chair by his workbench, Hanna pictures his expression, his resolute chin and full lower lip, and all at once she realizes who he looks like. She quickly flicks through the picture archives on the computer and finds confirmation of her impression. Steinn is the spitting image of the goldsmith from Bruges whom Jan van Eyck painted in the fifteenth century. He has a steadfast chin and a kindly face, gentle eyes and strong hands. No, not a goldsmith; an alchemist, Hanna thinks to herself, recalling Steinn's work with the most unlikely materials and tools, how he transforms devastation into beauty. Steinn at least is not the one who betrayed her; that much is certain.

9

LIGHT AND SHADE

The day Steinn returns to work, Edda buys a cake, which they all eat in the cafeteria before the gallery opens. Steinn has a patch over one eye, and Hanna immediately notices how different he is. More sure of himself than before, less fumbling, less stammering, and over coffee he laughs heartily and freely for the first time since she started work in January. The eye patch suits him.

The investigation into *The Birches* was put on hold when Steinn had his attack of acute glaucoma. He had an operation on his right eye and the left one will be done as a preventative measure. While Steinn was off work Hanna worked on the planning stages of the Annexe exhibitions. It is now well into March, and the exhibition, which Agusta planned before Hanna took on her post, is now upon them. This is part of Agusta's role with the international curators' group and includes artists from the Baltic countries, Finland, and Iceland.

The exhibitors are final-year students at the Academy of Arts; they were selected by Agusta and the Finnish curator, who has been staying in the visitors' apartment above the Annexe for the last two weeks. The curators' group is also showing their own works, and it was a real juggling act to get all the pieces to fit well together. The theme of the exhibition is how exhibition rooms and art museums have evolved to become community centers where boundaries between different branches of art intermingle and art as an academic subject is fading. The emphasis is on communication and education, not only for the general public, but also among scholars, and the Annexe has tried to forge links with the university by running lectures and discussion evenings.

The work has been enjoyable, and Hanna and Agusta have come to the conclusion that they have a lot in common. Now that Hanna knows about Kolbeinn, they also chat about their children. Hanna is itching to ask Agusta about Kolbeinn's father but Agusta is careful never to mention him by name, as if he doesn't exist, and Hanna is too considerate to ask her about something she doesn't want to talk about.

Any doubts that Hanna had at the outset about Agusta's capabilities have gradually given way to trust and gratitude for her drive and unstinting hard work. Agusta is resourceful and not easily stressed. She doesn't focus on problems but seeks solutions and has the knack of implementing them in a way that satisfies everyone. Agusta would do a good job as director of the Annexe, Hanna thinks to herself.

Baldur has kept his distance from Hanna. Politeness reigns between them, but Hanna is careful not to take him into her confidence. The friendliness that characterized their early interaction, which was based on their old friendship, disappeared like dew in the morning sun after that meeting. Agusta gives

Baldur support, but Hanna doesn't get involved and doesn't ask how the project is progressing.

The two events, the international landscape exhibition and Hanna's landscape exhibition, will open at the same time as the Arts Festival in Reykjavik, which of course is perfect from an artistic perspective and from the point of view of the gallery, but Hanna now suddenly finds herself with far less time to prepare. Leifur and Anselma haven't seen the need to keep her informed of their ideas until the last possible moment; they want to prepare part of their projects in situ, and this involves a degree of uncertainty that is hard to handle. One way for Hanna to contain her worries and anxiety is through exercise, and so she has gone back to the fencing piste again.

Hanna also used the time when Steinn was off to look into the idea that another painting, like *Composition in Blue*, might be under *The Birches*, and she came up with something significant. She is burning to let Steinn in on her discovery.

Now that they are sitting together over coffee Hanna can't help looking at him in surprise. The Steinn that she has known since she arrived is not at all the real Steinn, but the man who was ill, frightened, unsure, and convinced that he was going blind but couldn't bring himself to go to the doctor.

Steinn and Hanna are both visual people; they experience the beauty of life first and foremost through images, and for Steinn the thought of losing that must have been unbearable. And he was probably truly terrified at no longer being able to be the family's breadwinner; his pride was in tatters. Now he is a changed man. Directly after coffee he comes to her eagerly and with a gleam in his good eye. Hanna feels that for the first time she realizes how tall and well built Steinn is.

"I need to show you something," he says, as he had before, and they agree to meet in the basement later in the day. Walking down the stairs Hanna's heart is thumping with excitement. Now that Steinn is back Hanna feels at home in her work; he is invaluable to her, and she suspects she is not the only one in feeling that. Everyone has been unusually cheerful today.

Steinn goes straight to the computer and retrieves the picture, which he enlarges on the screen. Hanna waits to tell him about her discoveries. She puts down the book she was holding under her arm, a large book about the CoBrA painters. A folded sheet of paper is sticking out of it. Steinn shows her the screen.

"You see, I got the X-ray images of the painting before I went into the hospital. They are most informative."

Full of anticipation, Hanna looks at the image on the screen, and then she realizes to her disappointment that she cannot make head or tail of it. The image is in black-and-white, and dark shadows compete with lighter patches.

"This is the left half of the painting," Steinn explains. "The largest X-ray film at the hospital is forty-by-fifty centimeters, so we needed to do it in two sections."

Hanna gently puts her hand on Steinn's arm to stop him because she cannot make out what she is looking at on the screen.

"Steinn," she says slowly to calm him down as he is the excited one this time, unlike before when it was she who struggled to slow down to his tempo. "Can you just explain to me what we're looking at? What does this X-ray show? I didn't even know it was possible to take an X-ray of a painting at a hospital. So what are we seeing?"

Steinn looks at her, smiling; he is quite simply happy. He's in his element now, she thinks to herself.

"An X-ray is just an X-ray, no matter what it's of. You know that artists' paints, oil paints, always contain small amounts of heavy metals. And these metals are visible on an X-ray—that's why we can see these shapes so clearly here. OK, only black on white, or maybe white on black. The metals show up white on the X-ray."

Hanna looks at the black-and-white image on the screen, dark and light patches, but she doesn't see what he sees. To help her Steinn takes hold of the mouse and moves the cursor over the lines and shapes on the screen. After a while Hanna can make out half of the half-moon shape from the image.

"It's like the shapes you get in rock formations," she says. "Once you've seen a shape in a rock formation that's the way you always see it." And now she can also make out the diagonal stroke that breaks up the half-moon shape. Mentally rotating the image onto its side she is finally able to tell Steinn what she saw when he was lying unconscious on the floor and *Composition in Blue* was propped up against the wall directly in her line of vision.

"I didn't think it through then, but I'm absolutely one hundred percent certain that the paintings are exactly the same. I mean totally the same—d'you get what I'm saying? Not as if Sigfus had done a number of paintings with the same motif but with some variations, but like he'd simply painted two paintings that are identical. Don't you think that's strange? I don't get it. I've looked at many of Sigfus's paintings and read all the books there are about him, examined the data the gallery has and everything, but I've never come across two identical paintings."

Hanna doesn't voice what she is thinking; she doesn't need to. It has, of course, occurred to her that the gallery has not only been given a forgery attributed to Gudrun Johannsdottir, which *The Birches* almost certainly is, but also it could be that *Composition in Blue*, which the gallery was given the year before with so much jubilation, is a forgery. She doesn't mention it because it was Steinn who examined the painting at the time. He made a serious oversight and it is unnecessary to spell it out. Steinn makes no response.

"Turn it on its side a moment," Hanna asks, and Steinn rotates the image on the screen. He also brings up the other X-ray, rotates it, and puts them side by side. Finally he goes into the gallery's database and brings up a picture of *Composition in Blue* on the screen as well. He changes the settings on the image of the painting so it appears in black-and-white. Hanna follows his movements in silence. The similarity between the lines and shapes on the images is not only great; the structure is almost identical. Hanna looks at Steinn in triumph, but he just stares at the screen mumbling.

"Yep, this is what I suspected. I was thinking about this half-moon shape; Sigfus painted this a lot at the time."

"I've worked out what might have happened," says Hanna. She can't wait any longer. "Well, not who painted *The Birches*, but I realize that in fact it could be that *Composition in Blue* turned into *The Birches* when it was in Christian Holst's possession. When his estate released this painting it was in the same condition as it is now. I had the auction house send me a photograph. The picture fits exactly, but on their list the painter was down as unknown and the value was a mere fraction of the eight million Elisabet paid for it."

"That doesn't explain why the painting was changed, the trees, and the mountain? Did that also happen in Holst's time?" asks Steinn, but Hanna carries on without answering him.

"Holst bought up Elisabeth Hansen's entire collection. And I'm dead certain she bought a painting from Sigfus. I came across something when I was going through the records about Gudrun in the archives. They were friends, as you know, Sigfus and Gudrun."

"Surely you're not going to tell me that Gudrun painted over one of Sigfus's pictures?" Steinn asks, surprised and in disbelief.

"No, of course not," replies Hanna. "I still don't know who painted over the picture or altered it later. At the moment I'm only talking about how a painting by Sigfus could have got into Holst's possession."

Hanna reaches across for the large book lying on the table.

"First I found a letter in Gudrun's records, and then I started looking in books for pictures of Sigfus's from this period, until 1940. I also photocopied the letter Gudrun wrote; you must let me read it to you."

Crossing his arms, Steinn nods his head, waiting.

"Here's the letter," Hanna says. "Gudrun wrote it to her friend Mundi when he was in Italy. Just before he died. I find it so sad to think that they never met again. 'Copenhagen, October 15, 1938. My dear friend, The ladies in Nansens Street and I have been rather downcast since you, my dear friend, set off on your southern travels. The accordion lies untouched in the corner, and in your absence few make their way over here. I do hope that you recover soon, so that we may all sing together again, very shortly.

"'By the way, I went to an interesting party yesterday evening. Our friend, Sigfus, took me to a midweek soiree at Mrs. Hansen's; it is she who has purchased the many abstract paintings. At these soirees, selected artists are offered a free meal every Wednesday. Sigfus was invited on this occasion because Mrs. H assuredly wanted to buy a painting from him. She had seen it at an exhibition of abstract paintings where Sigfus was involved last summer—when we had our exhibition at home.

"'He was pleased to take me with him, but as you know, it is not anybody who is invited to Mrs. H's house, and she viewed me with displeasure even though dear Sigfus introduced me with enthusiasm. I was ready to walk straight back out, but he took me firmly by the arm.

"'Mrs. H is a queer one; you, my dear Mundi, could easily capture her expression—and her hair color, I wonder which chemist's shop that comes from? All the abstract painters you have heard about were there—Egill Jacobsen, of course, Ejler Bille and Carl-Henning Pedersen and others. And their paintings were displayed on every wall; her apartment is absolutely crammed with these paintings, full of animals, masks, and symbols. She didn't open the package with Sigfus's painting, just slipped it into the back room. Maybe she didn't want the others to know that she was buying from Sigfus; they are all as penniless as each other and all want to sell her their pictures. You should have seen how well we ate.

"'I don't always understand what their paintings mean, but abstract art fascinates me, although I don't have the courage for it yet. Some of the paintings are very memorable. When I look at my own landscape paintings, I see very little to recommend them. But that is what I'm doing at present, and we will see what the future holds. Sigfus was not bashful about the company. And they had plenty to talk about; I had to keep my wits about me to keep up because many of them spoke at once, largely about the possibility of war of course.'"

Hanna stops reading and hands Steinn the photocopy. She dries her eyes.

"They were such good friends and colleagues. Gudrun and Mundi, I mean."

"So you mean the butcher got Sigfus's painting included in the deal when he bought up Elisabeth Hansen's collection?" Steinn is pensive. "But why did it not turn up—oh no, of course. Someone painted over it. But who could that have been? When the painting was in his possession?" He shakes his head. "At any rate, Gudrun didn't do it."

"I think we can stop worrying about Gudrun," says Hanna. "She clearly isn't in any way linked to this. The question is what painting lies underneath. It's highly likely that it's by Sigfus. You can see that these paintings are almost identical," she says, looking at the screen.

"I saw a sketch of *Composition in Blue* at an exhibition in Copenhagen about two years ago," she adds. "There were also paintings by Gudrun. I was working on the exhibition with the Cultural Institute in Copenhagen and went to visit it. And the paintings by Sigfus from this period, around 1940, were very much in that style. *Composition in Blue* hadn't been found then, d'you remember? It was found with some people in Denmark a number of months later, wasn't it?"

"Yes, it was some family or other who owned the painting," replies Steinn. "It never emerged who bought it and donated it to the Icelandic state. Maybe it was only publicized over there—that could be. It was known that he did a painting from these sketches and called it *Composition in Blue.*"

Hanna gives him a meaningful look. Opening her book about the CoBrA painters she'd brought with her, she shows Steinn a small black-and-white picture.

"Look at this!" she says triumphantly.

Steinn looks at the picture. Then he takes the book over to his big workbench, and, laying it down, he reaches out for the magnifying lamp. Shining it onto the picture, he pores over the book. Then he straightens up, rubbing his good eye.

"Yes, I see what you mean."

Hanna goes over to the table and he hands her the magnifying glass; she examines the picture more carefully. It shows Sigfus Gunnarsson as a young man, Egill Jacobsen, and two other painters at a fine arts exhibition in a small gallery in Copenhagen in 1938. Egill later went on to become one of the CoBrA artists, and this was one of the first exhibitions he took part in. Various paintings are visible in the background; one of them is just like *Composition in Blue.*

Hanna and Steinn look at each other. There can be no doubt. It is extremely likely that the painting Elisabeth Hansen saw at the exhibition in 1938 and then bought from Sigfus was indeed the painting that looks remarkably like *Composition in Blue.* The date fits at any rate.

"Hold on a moment; this isn't all," says Hanna. "The butcher donated the majority of the collection he bought from Elisabeth to a museum on Jutland. The museum has a register of all the paintings that came from him. I got in touch with them and there is no painting by Sigfus Gunnarsson. So the butcher must have kept it."

"If he bought it in the first place," says Steinn. "But it's very likely, going by this."

"And what shall we do now?" asks Hanna.

"We just remove the top surface," says Steinn straight-out. He gets up to fetch *The Birches*, places it on his workbench, and pulls the angle lamp over, lighting up the painting completely. He rubs his good eye.

Hanna gives him a worried look.

"It's all right," says Steinn. "It's just because the patch on the other eye makes this one tired."

"Are you going to do it now?" Hanna asks, aghast. Steinn bursts out laughing.

"No, of course not. I don't even know if it's possible. It depends on the chemical makeup. I'll have to have a closer look."

They both look at the painting. Hanna does not see beauty in the brushstrokes, nor does she admire the interplay of colors on the canvas. She sees an embarrassing artifact, the fruit of greed and deceit that demeans art and Gudrun's work. But what if a genuine work of art lies hidden there, under the birch copse?

"But what about Gudrun's painting though?" asks Hanna without expecting an answer. "Should we give preference to a painting that could potentially be by a male artist over a genuine painting by a female artist? Is a work of art by Sigfus more important than one by Gudrun? She was just as talented an artist as Sigfus. How can we choose between them? We can't be a hundred percent sure that this isn't a painting by Gudrun."

Hanna isn't sure what the right thing to do is. In her mind she still hasn't excluded the possibility that this is Gudrun's painting. She feels she needs to protect women's interests, as women often do, consciously or unconsciously, in all fields. In the art world women are not on an equal footing with men any more than anywhere else, but Hanna doesn't want to go into that with Steinn, nor does it interest him. Steinn is clearly no chauvinist, no more than many other men. But he wouldn't see it as a gender issue. In his eyes Gudrun and Sigfus are equally important as painters, and that is enough for him.

Steinn doesn't respond immediately; instead he runs his finger lightly down the trunk of a birch in the copse. "Yes, you're right. The other option is to do nothing. Keep quiet about it. Exhibit *The Birches* as an original by Gudrun." Steinn hesitates. He looks at the gnarled birch in the painting. He carries on, his voice not entirely free of sarcasm. "That would suit everyone nicely. We would avoid the hassle. It would also be better for the gallery. Better for Elisabet Valsdottir. Better for the auction house. For the person who forged this. Maybe better for everyone apart from Gudrun Johannsdottir, and she is dead."

Hanna notices a small vertical wrinkle appear in the middle of Steinn's forehead as it always does when he is dissatisfied with something.

"It would be best for everyone," he goes on. "Silence is golden. Why do you think that the forgery case just fizzled out and all these paintings are back in circulation? Precisely for this reason—people don't want to know about it. It's much safer just to turn a blind eye to a Kjarval painting bought at auction for three million. Why have it investigated just to discover it is worthless? None of your friends can tell the difference anyway. Everyone is in on it. Even the auction house. Do you think that we'll ever find out who bought the painting from the man's estate and sold it on when Elisabet bought it?"

Steinn is angry.

"Or even when *Composition in Blue* was bought last year. I'll tell you about that one. It was one of the most expensive works of art by an Icelandic artist that had ever been purchased. It was in all the papers. But do you think I get to see the ownership history?"

Steinn turns his gaze from the painting to Hanna, his eye flaming with fury; she has never seen him so enraged before.

"No, it wasn't released. As you know. No one knows who found the painting housed by a family from Denmark who put it up for auction, where the bank bought it." He shakes his head. "I'd always intended to look more closely into this family in Denmark who were supposed to have found the work. I still haven't got around to it. My eyes were acting up at the time."

"Why isn't this information released?" asks Hanna. "I don't understand it. It's not as if it's personal or medical details—I could understand that. But of course it's obvious what's behind it."

Steinn nods in agreement. "Maybe someone needed to dispose of black-market money or simply wants to keep their private business private."

Hanna gazes at the painting, looking for something to reveal the deceit, something that shows beyond doubt that the painting cannot have been by Gudrun, but obviously there is nothing to give it away.

"We need to discuss this with Kristin," says Steinn calmly, "before we do anything."

Hanna gives a sigh of relief. So she doesn't need to take the plunge herself and potentially destroy a work of art by one of the nation's most distinguished female artists.

"I'm also going to send a paint sample up to the university for analysis," says Steinn. "Then we can determine the age of the colors better. Best to take a sample from *Composition in Blue* while I'm at it. That could have been forged from the outset. Painted on an old canvas, secured on an old frame, and then the colors made to look authentic. Forgers actually seek out paintings in an artist's career that are known about but haven't yet been found. Then the painting suddenly 'appears' and matches precisely what was known about it. But we'd better discuss this with Kristin as quickly as possible. Preferably right now. This is a serious issue, and it shouldn't wait."

Hanna detects a newfound confidence in his words, a focus and decisiveness that she likes.

"But can we be absolutely sure?" The danger seems great to Hanna. "A work of art by Gudrun, or not by her, cost eight million. And then to say, let's wash it off. Even though it may be covering a painting by Sigfus. We need to be certain."

"We will be," replies Steinn bluntly, and he turns off the computer. "We'll get this settled when the analysis comes through."

Hanna stands up; she needs to move.

"Forgeries have certainly been on the increase in the last few years. I was reading up about it while you were off work." She doesn't say *sick*; that word doesn't suit Steinn. "Not long ago even Sotheby's withdrew a painting by Shishkin the day before it was due to be put up for auction."

"Yes, that's right," says Steinn. "You're talking serious money there."

"Why do we need to run this by Kristin? Wouldn't it be better to have something specific before we talk to her?"

"But we've already got something," replies Steinn. "The paint sample would really only be a confirmation of what we know—*The Birches* is a forgery."

Hanna feels a stab in her heart hearing him say it straight-out like that. They both know that Kristin will not be pleased to hear that the painting her friend Elisabet gave her is a worthless forgery. The only upside could be that under the forgery lies a work that is probably by Sigfus Gunnarsson. Especially if the painting by Sigfus the gallery already owns also turns out to be a forgery.

"Elisabet would have done better putting the money into research," says Hanna sarcastically. "That way we might be in a better position now."

Steinn switches off the lamp and wraps *The Birches* back up. "We'll see if we can get a hold of Kristin before she goes. Best to get the deed over with," he says, smiling encouragingly at Hanna.

It's late in the day and the gallery has already closed. When Hanna and Steinn get up to Kristin's office, it has begun to grow dark outside and the snow-covered sides of Mount Esja are a reddish pink; the sun is beginning to dip in the sky. Hanna looks out over the familiar lines of the mountain as she has so often since she arrived, and yet again feels happy to be home, despite Frederico's affair and missing her family and despite this unexpected turn her job has taken. Mount Esja is also her mountain; she doesn't feel fond of it in the way she does of the mountains from her childhood, but Esja is still part of her life. She would love the mountains to be part of Heba's life as well, but she knows she will have to accept that they never will be. Heba doesn't hold mountains in her soul, she thinks almost reverently. She holds the city, canals, buildings, and the hustle and bustle of urban life.

Steinn has sat down, and Kristin is looking inquiringly at Hanna.

"I'm sorry," says Hanna. "The view from here is always so beautiful."

Steinn looks at Hanna silently, and she begins telling Kristin the whole story. Kristin leans back in her chair, giving Hanna her full attention; she doesn't interrupt but waits patiently. When Hanna has finished Kristin looks her straight in the eye, and Hanna sees the glitter of steel.

"This is pure speculation," says Kristin. She looks at them in turn. "It's out of the question. We're talking about a work of art worth millions. A national treasure. You both know how important Gudrun Johannsdottir is to us. We can't prove this. What is to be gained by destroying this painting? And if it does prove to be a forgery, we've everything to lose. You both know the effect this will have on her other works of art we own. Are we to investigate them all?"

She shakes her head. Hanna realizes she will not be budged.

"The Icelandic fine arts market is only now finding its feet again after that forgery case sent it reeling. This would trigger more unease. And Elisabet wouldn't want to bring charges— I know that for sure. She is quite an art connoisseur and she bought this piece herself. She wouldn't want the press claiming that she'd bought a forgery."

Hanna stares dumbfounded at Kristin.

"Hanna dear," adds Kristin. "You must understand the position we're in. It's such a small world here, such a volatile one. We just can't do this as things stand, not right now, you understand. We'll keep the lid on it for a while, look into it more. I'm not saying no. I'm just suggesting not now. Let's give it further consideration."

Hanna is about to protest, but Kristin cuts in.

"I'll give Elisabet a call and tell her that the investigation into her painting is taking longer than we anticipated. She'll understand. Let's shelve it for a while."

Hanna perceives that Kristin is clearly as hard as iron. Despite her words about shelving it and careful consideration, Hanna has zero expectation that she will agree to removing the top layer from the painting later on. But there is evidently no point in trying to discuss the issue. They make ready to leave.

"We won't discuss this any further," says Steinn politely.

Kristin glances at her watch, and they say good-bye. They are in the doorway when Kristin calls, "Steinn? Have you got a moment?"

Steinn turns back. Hanna pauses.

"We'll see you tomorrow, Hanna dear," says Kristin, smiling warmly, like a totally different person, as if the discussion had not taken place. Hanna nods and walks down the corridor toward the stairs. Behind her she can hear Steinn's voice as he goes back into Kristin's office. He lowers his voice, and Hanna stops at the top stair straining to hear, but she cannot make anything out, just the sound of the door closing.

1 0

WORKSHOP FOR YOUNG OFFENDERS

The teenagers came escorted by a social worker and are now standing in a huddle in the Annexe. Uneasy, Hanna waits for Agusta; she has more confidence in her ability to relate to them. Agusta is no more than a few years older than the oldest ones. Hanna is only interested in one member of the group, but she doesn't show it and avoids looking at Kari any more than the others. She recognized him immediately; he is by far the smallest. Brown-haired, with hazel eyes, darting like a skittish animal. She knows nothing about him other than that he's thirteen, the police caught him along with the other youngsters for illegal graffitiing, and the child social work team is actively involved in his case.

Hanna has seen what these kids are capable of, the vandalism they have done, for example, on the statue she and Steinn visited. She also managed to have a picture sent to her of the piece Kari did on the wall where he was caught recently. She cannot forget that wall; it's as if a slow explosion was taking place in the picture, at once full of pain and passion. Hanna hopes to be able to show Kari that you can give expression to such a powerful artistic urge in other ways, even though the destructive urge is as strong as the creative one. The photo of that wall showed her that there's a powerful force within Kari and if he could learn to harness it he could do amazing things. Otherwise he will burn up in a flash, like a firework that leaves no trace other than smoke in the darkness.

Gudny proved to be more influential than Hanna had expected; it was only a few days after their lunchtime meeting in the restaurant that she got in touch with Hanna.

"I've sorted it for you," she said. "The kids can come to you whenever you want. You just need to get in touch with Ingunn at Social Services and she will arrange for them to come over to you. Just name the day. You also need to talk to her about the bill, but keep it low, expenses only sort of thing." Hanna agreed straightaway and thanked her, without having a clue what she was going to do with a group of teenagers for a whole Saturday. She has never worked with teenagers before, and she doesn't know any Icelandic youngsters other than her relatives, whom she hardly ever sees. She's only seen teenagers on the street from a distance, wandering neglected around the town, and she feels they must be cold the whole time.

Now here they are, five of them in total, and all looking like they'd rather be someplace else. Hanna suspects that this last-minute art workshop courtesy of the Reykjavik city authorities is a punishment rather than a reward. Three boys and two girls. Kari is like a mascot for this group, who are all older than him. The two girls are dressed in identical tight-legged jeans, whispering. Hanna guesses they are about fourteen or fifteen. The older boys have long hair with their pants hanging around their knees. None of them looks her in the eye. Kari is looking around, and Hanna notices he has seen a painting by a student at the Art Academy. The painting drips down the wall and onto the floor, a thread of red paint connecting the space. She is convinced he wants to look at it more but is holding himself back, probably determined not to show any reaction or interest, no matter what.

Hanna has introduced herself and has talked about famous graffiti artists like Banksy and Blek le Rat. They listened half-heartedly; one girl was constantly on her phone texting and undoubtedly hearing nothing of what Hanna was saying, but that doesn't bother Hanna. It's Kari she wants to get through to. It's him she wants to save, to arouse his interest in art, get him off the streets like Tim Rollins did in his work with the Kids of Survival project back in the 1980s, kids from a poor part of New York. He showed that it was possible to reach out to kids through literature, music, and art, kids the schools had written off as hopeless.

But Hanna is no Tim Rollins, and she has no idea how to reach out to these youngsters who, at best, appear disinterested. She outlines for them what they are going to do that day. They'll start by looking around the Annexe and the gallery, and then they can have a free hand in the small exhibition space on the upper floor, which is empty at present. Steinn has given his blessing for them to paint on the walls, but they'll have wall paint and brushes rather than spray cans. The gallery would then be honored to display their work and they are welcome to come back and finish it if they don't manage to today.

Hanna sighs with relief when she sees Agusta walking across the square outside; she takes over when Hanna has finished her talk. Hanna feels the group listens to Agusta better. It's easy for her to talk on their level without it sounding contrived. Coming from her mouth words like *the crew*, *doing a piece*, *writers*, and *taggers* sound totally natural, as if she was one of them. Hanna leaves Agusta to guide the group through the works on display in the Annexe. The girls whisper to one another, and the boys talk in undertones. Kari looks out of the windows. Then Hanna takes over; they've had enough of being talked to about art. For them graffitiing isn't art; in their eyes graffitiing is something that is banned, an exciting way to make their presence felt.

Hanna leads them up to the next floor, where paintings from the first half of the twentieth century are in a display entitled *Initiators*—portraits, still lifes, street scenes, and paintings of Reykjavik's harbor. These paintings are accessible and easy to understand, but Hanna sees that the kids are bored; they want to leave and are simply waiting for the workshop to be over. It's a Saturday and should be a day off. None of them wants to waste it indoors in a gallery. They have never heard of Thorvald Skulason or Gunnlaug Blondal, or Gudrun Johannsdottir either. Hanna gets no response from them, and there is clearly an unspoken agreement among them not to show any interest in anything to do with the gallery. Hanna sends Agusta a pleading look, but she just shrugs with an expression that says: Well, what did you expect? Hanna has no answer to that, and eventually she takes them down to the ground floor, where she hopes they will relate better to the exhibition of contemporary photographs.

On the stairs Hanna walks straight past *Composition in Blue*, but one of the older kids stops dead in his tracks.

"Hey! I saw this on TV last year. It cost fifteen mill." They crowd around the painting.

"Fifteen million?" the others exclaim. "Wow, man!"

They look at one another, and suddenly Hanna has their undivided attention.

"The guy who painted this, is he dead?" Kari asks. Hanna confirms this with a nod, thinking to herself that if she and Steinn are right then the artist, whoever he is, is probably very comfortably off somewhere.

"Then who gets the money?" he asks.

Seizing the moment, Hanna explains to them how paintings are bought and sold and tells them how much some of the paintings in the gallery are worth, the most expensive ones she can remember. Now they show more interest; maybe art isn't entirely dumb. Hanna keeps them focused by talking about the vast sums paid for works of art on the world market, and about artists who have become megarich like Damien Hirst and Jeff Koons. She sees that Kari is listening. He probably lives on the breadline and dreams of living in luxury.

"We have one internationally famous artist," says Hanna. "He's almost as famous as Bjork. His works can cost tens or even hundreds of millions." Hanna tells the kids about Olafur Eliasson, and while she talks she looks at *Composition in Blue* and is actually certain she is right. This is a forgery even though it doesn't look it.

She knows Steinn has taken a sample. He said nothing about his discussion with Kristin after Hanna left, but she gets the feeling he hasn't given up. Now they are just waiting for the results.

Agusta calls out and startles Hanna. She was lost in thought looking at the painting and the group has moved on down to the ground floor. The ice is now broken, and the youngsters relate better to the photographs than the paintings on the upper floor. They keep coming up with questions, mostly about how much they are worth but also about how artists work. Who gets to exhibit in the gallery, how they are chosen, and whether they get paid. They like the freedom that artists have, that they can get on with their work when they please and aren't at someone's beck and call. Hanna doesn't disillusion them, and it's also true to an extent. She sees no reason to quash their interest in art or their dreams of freedom by pointing out to them how few artists succeed in making a living out of their art, and that even fewer get international recognition. She memorizes their names, and when they go to eat in the cafeteria she carefully probes them about their graffitiing. She regrets it immediately. Their faces go blank; they look away and start texting again. Hanna sees Agusta look at her in amazement, and she knows she's put her foot in it. She just doesn't have the knack.

After lunch Hanna lets Agusta take the group up to the room they have at their disposal. Steinn has put plastic sheeting down on the floor. They can have one wall for themselves, and they can do whatever they like on it. Hanna has decided to leave Agusta on her own with them while they get started. She blames herself for not relating to them better than she did. She would love to talk to Kari, but she knows he would shrink back so it's better to give him time. That's why she remains in the cafeteria for a while. On the table in front of her there's a printout of one of the first political murals in history, *Allegory of Good Government and Bad Government*, which are on the walls of the town hall in Sienna. She'd intended to show it to the youngsters.

At the request of the town councilors, Ambrogio Lorenzetti painted the frescoes on the walls of their council room in the early part of the fourteenth century. They cover a number of square meters and show the effects of good government versus poor government on town and countryside. In the allegory of good government well-dressed people walk about on clean, tidy streets; the houses are in good repair; and there's a plentiful harvest in the country. It goes without saying that the opposite is the case under bad government: houses are in disrepair, beggars and paupers are out on the streets, the countryside is neglected, and the harvest is poor. Hanna is wondering whether she should go up and show the pictures to the youngsters when Steinn suddenly appears.

"I thought you wanted to be up with the kids?" says Steinn, surprised. He's still got his eye patch. Hanna looks at his good eye and shows him the pictures in the folder.

"I was going to show them these. But I'm not sure it's a good idea." She flicks through the pictures with him.

"Why not?" asks Steinn. "It might get them started; I don't think they know what they're meant to be doing up there."

Hanna lets out a sigh; she needs to get a grip. Steinn is standing behind her and lays his hand on her shoulder. She doesn't move; she thinks of Frederico. Pulling herself together, she suddenly stands up and gathers up the pictures on the table.

Steinn smiles at her, and Hanna feels the attraction toward him. She's not sure if Steinn feels the same way. It has occurred to her that maybe she should give Frederico a dose of his own medicine for what he did, but she doesn't have the courage. Besides, she wants to keep her friendship with Steinn. A love affair at work is not what she needs. She takes her leave of Steinn and his inscrutable gaze and rushes up to the painting room.

Everything is quiet and calm. Agusta has slipped off, and the five youngsters are sitting on the floor. They've opened the paint cans but can't agree on how they should paint the wall. Hanna says hello, and they fall silent and look at her, waiting. She feels she is interrupting them, but then she thinks about fencing and how it is important to take the initiative. Sitting down next to them, she spreads out the pictures of *Good Government and Bad Government* on the floor. None of them has been to Sienna, and Hanna tells them about the time she went there with Frederico and Heba some years ago.

"Walls encircle the old town center, which is up on a hill, surrounded by other hills."

Hanna tells them about the afternoon they spent with their friends in the hills. There was a warm breeze, and the cherry trees in the orchard were laden with berries. The hills were green, and on the neighboring farm there was a foal in the meadow. Heba went with some of the children to collect water from the well.

"It was a glorious day," says Hanna dreamily, picturing the grassy meadows and fruit trees, recalling the gentle peace that reigned over everything that day. She looks at Kari and sees that he is listening.

"The following day we drove into Sienna," she says, "and parked the car right outside the city walls. Then we had to take seven escalators to get up to the old town center. We came out onto streets that are so narrow you can touch the houses on either side if you stretch your arms right out. A real horse race is held in the town center twice a year. Thousands of people come from all over the world to watch *Il Palio*. The town hall in Sienna is on this square, and that's where you can find this fresco.

"Artists often want to express something in their art, maybe something in their environment that they're dissatisfied with. Although that wasn't the case with Lorenzetti here—he was commissioned to paint this."

They examine the pictures and have a bit of a laugh at the primitive way the perspective on the buildings has been drawn and at the angels in midflight. But it also gives them a subject matter, and when one of the girls asks if she can paint an angel on the wall, Hanna agrees enthusiastically, relieved that one of them wants to get involved. The girls begin drawing on the wall in chalk, and Hanna immediately sees that they can't cope with the size of the wall. She goes to find Agusta.

With Steinn's help they produce a computer and an overhead projector; now they can project whatever they want onto the wall and paint the outlines. They potter about with this for a good while; when the computer arrived it was like the kids came to life. They now try to come to an agreement about their subject matter, angels, buildings, and people. Hanna notices that Kari doesn't get involved; he's not interested, and the others don't look to him. She wonders what his role is in the group. He sits with his back to the wall, his face expressionless, and Hanna risks sitting down next to him.

"What would you do if you had a whole wall to yourself?" she asks nonchalantly, as if to no one in particular, making sure to avoid eye contact.

She senses rather than sees him shrug his shoulders indifferently; he doesn't look up but, shaking his head, replies coldly, "Dunno."

Hanna sits quietly without saying another word, but Kari gets straight up and goes over to the others. Gradually they decide on the pictures and draw the outlines on the wall, outlines of American skyscrapers with angels flying over them. One of the boys takes it on himself to sketch out a skate park, and Hanna and Agusta advise them where best to start, how to work the background and work with colors on the wall. They've been contentedly doing this for some time when Hanna notices that Kari is no longer there but has silently slipped off without a word. She gets up and goes right down to the lobby. She is halfway down the stairs when she hears voices and shouting.

"Hey, you there!"

Hanna gets to the bottom just in time to see Kari aim a can of red paint and splatter it over the floor and up the wall by the entrance. Then he takes to his heels and is away. Hanna's first thought is that it's just as well it wasn't a work of art that suffered the explosion of paint, and then she remembers the question that he shrugged off.

11

MY FRIEND BANKSY

Kari is holding a spray can and spraying a gray wall in white paint. In his dream the wall is huge and so is he; he hears the hiss of the can and smells the glossy odor—he loves this smell. He covers the wall, the coarse gray concrete, with white spray that veils everything, hides every flaw; he is on a high, high on a white cloud. Behind him he hears someone gently calling his name, and when he turns around Banksy is standing there in a hoodie and a monkey mask. Kari knows it's him; he sees his smiling eyes looking with satisfaction at the white covering Kari is bombing over the wall. Enveloped in the cool softness of the white cloud, Kari is bursting with joy and happiness; it is glorious and he wants to stay floating there forever. He looks Banksy in the eye; they are friends, fellow graffitists. Then Banksy lifts up both hands in a sign of peace and floats up into the air and disappears, vanishing into the white spray-paint.

Immediately Kari feels something hard under his chest, and a powerful smell of urine and vomit penetrate his senses. He is ice-cold, shivering, and feels sick. Someone is trying to turn him on the hard concrete floor in the pool of mess, trying to get to his pockets. He lies motionless; underneath him the spray can is hurting him, but he doesn't move. There's nothing in his pockets, not even a cigarette, and he lies still until the foul-smelling person stops fumbling. No one from the crew is there; they have left. Kari doesn't open his eyes but lies there on his stomach on the floor, trying to think of the white cloud again and the blissful feeling he had in his dream, but he knows it won't come back, not until next time.

12

SEJA MARGINAL, SEJA HEROI

Scraps of wood, rusty corrugated iron, tar-coated particle board, and glass lie heaped on the floor of the Annexe and there's another pile on the pavement outside, visible through the glass. It is well into May and the heat inside is tropical, rather like Brazil, native country to Helio Oiticica, the artist who effortlessly bridged the gap between modernism and open environmental installations in which the viewer plays an integral role. More often than not these were constructed from incidental materials in the artist's everyday environment. Oiticica also bridged the gap between South and North America, between the favelas of Rio de Janeiro and the affluent areas of New York and London; his art appeals to young and old alike. He died before his time, in 1980, before Leifur was born, but nevertheless he is one of Leifur's heroes. *Seja marginal, seja heroi* was one of his slogans, which Leifur can well envisage adopting as his own. *Be courageous, live on the edge.*

Leifur is alone in the room; he doesn't notice the heat. The sun has been shining in through the glass roof all night; now it's shining in through the windows overlooking the square, and the shadows of the window frames form lines on the gray tiled floor, which looks almost white in the bright sunlight. Apart from Leifur's scraps of wood, there are only Haraldur's paintings in the room, wrapped in brown paper and leaning up against the end wall. Leifur is careful not to come near them, but apart from that he is in a world of his own. He is creating his art in situ.

He has been collecting materials since January and storing them in his friend's garage. He has conscientiously chosen rusted sheets of corrugated iron, wood, and discarded building materials according to their shape, size, color, and texture. Leifur lets the sculpture, as he calls the configuration of items, spread out around the exhibition space and onto the street, like looking through a mirror on the wall. The heap on the pavement outside is neatly marked *art gallery*, but twice yesterday Hanna had to stop the street cleaners from clearing away the timber.

Leifur is absorbed in his work and doesn't notice Haraldur coming in. He leans a sheet of corrugated iron, reddish-brown with rust, on a pillar near the window and works his way from there, angling pieces of wood, which at one time had been painted blue, up against the iron sheeting, thus making it the focal point of the piece. He paces up and down, muttering to himself, whereas Haraldur stands motionless in the doorway, not saying a word. The heat in the room hits him like a wave. Only the two of them have turned up. Today is the first day they can install their work for the exhibition *Landscape: Past and Present*. Anselma and Jon haven't arrived yet, and Hanna is in a meeting.

Hanna let Leifur in when he arrived that morning; he was waiting at the door. She'd picked up on his eager vibes, his total concentration, and the tension enveloping him like a veil of static. She didn't see Haraldur walking across the square, looking at them both from a distance, nor how he eyed the heap of building materials outside the exhibition space. And she didn't see his disgruntled gait, which was at odds with the warmth of the morning sun. Hanna has gone off to a meeting with Baldur and Kristin and isn't expected back just yet. But Edda is there, and she comes up behind Haraldur as he stands in the doorway, looking at the bits of garbage spread out just where he had planned to put up his paintings.

"If you need anything, just let me know," she says to them both, but neither of them hears her; Leifur is absorbed in his work, and Haraldur is watching him.

"I'll go and make you some coffee," says Edda, hurrying off.

Haraldur steps into the room as if the floor were dirty and he needed to be careful not to lose his footing. For a moment he is at a loss, like a sportsman walking onto the pitch who realizes he is out of condition. Haraldur knew what Leifur was planning, but he hadn't envisaged a work of this magnitude awaiting him in the exhibition room. As well as Leifur's installation, there is Jon's work to consider; at least Anselma intends to set up her work outside the gallery. Her design, a work of art in the public space that integrates passersby, was totally lost on Haraldur. He's not interested in trying to fathom such an idea and doesn't believe it has anything to do with art. Jon hasn't given away much about what he is going to exhibit. They're not expecting him until tomorrow, and he hasn't sent anything over.

Treading cautiously over to his paintings, Haraldur tosses a chilly greeting to Leifur. Leifur looks up, nods indifferently, and carries on with his work. Haraldur is offended by this lack of respect from a young artist, and he expresses this slightly by clearing his throat. He is also displeased that Hanna isn't available. Haraldur belongs to that generation of artists who takes it for granted that someone else, the curator or gallery director, will make the decisions about hanging the paintings and the layout of the display. He feels it's Hanna's job. Or at least their joint decision, and he doesn't feel comfortable doing it without her. Haraldur is down on all fours, removing the wrapping paper from his paintings, when Edda reappears and puts a tray of coffee down on the floor.

"Just shout if you need anything else," she says. "Hanna will be along shortly."

Haraldur gets up and pours himself a coffee. He would really like to sit down, but there aren't any chairs. Leifur also walks over to the coffeepot and silently pours himself a cup. He virtually ignores Haraldur as he paces around and around what looks to Haraldur like a heap of garbage. He is frowning, and then Anselma appears with her computer bag slung over her shoulder. Haraldur gives her a dark look, but Leifur doesn't even notice her.

"Good morning," she says politely, taking a seat on the floor by the coffee tray as she would at home.

"I thought you were going to be somewhere outside, amongst the passersby," says Haraldur with a hint of scorn. His words indicate his view of artists who continually seek to follow the newest international trends and movements. Anselma doesn't let his manner bother her, or maybe his disparaging comments are lost on her because of her limited command of Icelandic. In any case, she just gives Haraldur a friendly smile and silently watches Leifur working. Haraldur senses that despite her politeness she is ignoring him. Not for the first time he is cross with himself for getting involved with this exhibition. On the surface he has appeared tolerant, but inside he is seething. The heat in the room does nothing to improve his mood, but he doesn't take off his coat.

Hanna's invitation was the first sign of interest anyone had shown in his work for over ten years, and that is a long time in an artist's career.

Now he thinks the whole thing is a complete mistake. What is he doing here with these young fools who don't know what painting is? They haven't battled as he has. They haven't experienced the hatred and contempt he and his like-minded contemporaries and colleagues had to endure just five decades ago, when they were showered with abuse on the streets, when abstract art was considered to be in the worst taste, a crime against art and against society. And now they call this art, he thinks, hurt and angry, looking out at Leifur's pile of junk out on the street that the passersby have to sidestep.

Haraldur thumps his coffee mug down and turns to his paintings. He has nothing to say to these youngsters, and clearly they have nothing to say to him. When he was young he showed respect for those who had gone before, paved the way. I doubt this Leifur realizes he wouldn't be here with this garbage of his if abstract artists hadn't fought his battles long ago. They taught people to see, to look and think, he grumbles to himself. But Leifur sees nothing but the rusty sheet of corrugated iron, which he is carrying like a baby, and sets down carefully only to pick it up again even more carefully and rear-range it.

Haraldur does his utmost to calm down. He has a habit of losing his temper and it has happened to him before, but not for a long time. He now starts to slowly remove the wrapping from his paintings. Anselma is still sitting at her computer screen. Haraldur glances at her and Leifur, but neither of them is watching him or showing any interest in his paintings. He tries not to let it bother him; he wants to maintain his dignity. When he has finished unwrapping all the paintings, he folds the paper up and suddenly a mischievous idea pops into his head. He picks the papers up and walks over to Leifur.

"Maybe I can offer you this as well?" he asks. "And here's a bit of string."

Haraldur is standing there, stiff with ill-disguised contempt in front of Leifur, who looks at him politely, not realizing that Haraldur is mocking him.

"Er, what? No, I, um, er? What? I didn't bring this," he says abstractedly. Then he turns away from Haraldur and carries on shuffling around with his sheet of corrugated iron.

Haraldur stands motionless, the wind taken out of his sails. Now anger takes over. His hands are shaking as he walks away, but on the surface he appears completely calm. He turns his back to Leifur and stares at his paintings up against the wall, as if he's working out where to hang them, but he sees nothing, only red.

He turns abruptly on his heel and Anselma looks up at the sudden movement. Haraldur walks without hesitation past the sheet of corrugated iron that Leifur has just finished setting up very carefully against the radiator near the window; he sticks his foot out a fraction. The iron sheeting clatters to the ground, taking the pane of glass with it, which shatters loudly onto the tiles. They all give a start, even Haraldur although he was responsible. From outside comes the sound of footsteps and the door opens.

Hanna and Edda stand astonished in the doorway as Leifur turns on the old man in a flash, grabs him by his collar, and pins him up against the glass wall. Out on the street passersby stop to watch anxiously.

"What the hell were you thinking, Haraldur? Can't you see what I'm doing here?"

Leifur's voice is gruff but barely raised, and he lets go of Haraldur as quickly as he started. He turns away and is about to walk off when Haraldur takes a step forward, grabs him by the shoulder, and turns him around. Pulling him up close, Haraldur lands a resounding blow on Leifur's jaw so he loses his balance and falls on the broken glass scattered over the floor. Leifur's cheekbone bangs onto the tiles and fragments of glass, and he cuts his cheek; the blood trickles down his jaw as he sits sharply back up and stares openmouthed at Haraldur, who is standing over him, red-faced and panting. Leifur tries to stand up but suddenly goes deathly white and crashes straight back down onto the floor.

Edda and Hanna see that Leifur has also cut his hand. Edda calls for an ambulance. Hanna runs over to Leifur and crouches down beside him, and Haraldur sweeps out the door. Someone on the street calls out to him, but he doesn't respond; he just strides rapidly across the square and disappears out of sight.

13

UNDER THE BIRCH TREES

"He said it was owned by a Danish farmer on Mon," Hanna says to Steinn. It's a quiet morning at the gallery and she is sitting at his workbench, supposedly studying the repair reports. She has one of them in front of her now; the vandalism is still going on. Since the young offenders workshop she feels the attacks are directed specifically at her. As if she was responsible. She hasn't tried to get in touch with Kari again after the incident that day, but she often thinks about him. She understands him, in retrospect. Why did she think she could arouse his interest in art in just one day?

The floor tiles in the lobby had to be partially replaced. Kristin wasn't unduly sympathetic though she didn't say anything. Hanna has less leeway now than she did when she started, and the landscape exhibition booklet that she had underway is suddenly not going to be published.

"The fund-raising didn't go as well as we'd hoped," said Kristin by way of explanation and simply pointed out the obvious fact that the exhibition Baldur is organizing in conjunction with Herbert Grunewald will take up a lot of the funds the gallery has available this year. Relations between Hanna and Kristin have generally been somewhat cooler since their talk about *The Birches*.

Steinn is free of his eye patch. He watches Hanna, and she looks at his eyes rather than into them, looking for telltale signs of the operation.

"If you look carefully you can see a black triangle on the iris, right on the edge," says Steinn, a smile playing at the corners of his mouth. Hanna looks hard and finally spies a black mark.

"Oh yes," she says, then looks back at the report. Steinn no longer shrinks away from contact with her as he did when she first started, when she almost always felt that he thought she was invading his space. Now it's the other way around; if they accidently touch it's Hanna who pulls away.

"In Monaco, the tax haven?" he says eventually when they break eye contact.

"It would be really rather more appropriate if a dubious painting had come from there, wouldn't it? But it's not that Mon, but the Danish Mon. An island in southern Denmark."

"Of course, what was I thinking?" Steinn smiles. His smiles are not so rare now and they suit him well. "Where did you get that from?"

"From the auction house," replies Hanna.

They are talking about the first owner of *Composition in Blue*, the painting the gallery was given and that cost fifteen million.

"I met a very ordinary guy who gave out the information just like that, but maybe it's because the man's dead. He was a farmer near some town called Elmelunde."

"Dead, you say?" asks Steinn. "How convenient!" he says sarcastically, and Hanna agrees.

"So you think so, too! Of course, they didn't tell me who bought the painting from him and put it up for auction, where it sold for fifteen million. But the farmer is said to have bought the painting from Sigfus at an exhibition in Copenhagen before the war."

"I don't suppose there's anything on record about that transaction? A register of the exhibits, a list of purchasers, or something?" asks Steinn.

Hanna shakes her head. "No, I asked. Nothing along those lines. But what occurred to me," she says, lowering her voice because at that moment Edda walks in, "is that if *Composition in Blue* is a complete forgery then the forger could obviously have looked at the same books I have. Found the same picture. He could have based his painting on the picture in the book. That's why the picture and the painting are so alike. It would also explain why they're not the same size. There's nothing in Sigfus's sketches to indicate how big *Composition in Blue* was."

Steinn doesn't respond. Hanna knows he is not pleased that he was fooled by the painting when it came into the gallery's possession.

"It's obviously extremely well done if it is a forgery," she adds.

"We'll start tonight," says Steinn, suddenly decisive.

Hanna is taken aback. "Don't we need to look into it more? The man must have some descendants, a wife or children, someone who can tell us about this purchase, surely? Or, if we're right, that he didn't buy the painting."

"A farmer down on Mon isn't exactly a likely candidate to buy a painting by Sigfus Gunnarsson," says Steinn brusquely, and Hanna senses a wall of stubbornness from him and sees the look of indignation on his face. "We've come to our conclusion," he says. "We'll talk about it again tonight."

Hanna hesitates. What would Frederico advise? She hasn't mentioned any of this to him; their conversations are still brief and revolve almost entirely around Heba. From her contact with Heba though Hanna has realized that Frederico is very keen to make up for what happened. And, after the conversation with Laufey, Hanna's anger toward Frederico has receded. Their marriage has been the cornerstone of her life for almost two decades.

Frederico would probably tell her to follow her gut instincts; that's what he's always done. And she gave Steinn her word. She can't let him down now; she can't pull out and withdraw. It's too late for that. After a moment's silence she takes the initiative to end the conversation and puts her hand on the reports on the table. Then, picking up the papers, she stands up and walks away. Mentally she unsheathes her foil, but she is scared and has trouble holding it steady; her arm isn't strong. If they've got it wrong, if there's an entirely different painting underneath *The Birches* and not *Composition in Blue*, then her future is in jeopardy. She would undoubtedly lose her job, and so would Steinn. She would lose her reputation. Maybe they would both lose their jobs even if they were right. Then all of a sudden Hanna remembers what she'd forgotten to ask Steinn.

"What did Kristin want with you the other day?"

"She was just asking how I was," he replies calmly, almost coolly, and Hanna can tell he doesn't want to talk about it. She doesn't believe him. Kristin could have asked Steinn how he was with Hanna there. Clearly he doesn't want to discuss this.

"How about we go over this tonight?" he asks, putting his hand next to hers on top of the report as if he meant the reports on the table. She looks down at his fingers and slides her hand away. Her eyes wander out the window, and she avoids looking Steinn in the eye. Her head is in turmoil, but then she regains her composure. She nods in agreement; she isn't going to back out.

When it comes time to do it, she is uneasy. Steinn is waiting in the basement, but the painting is nowhere to be seen. "Best to be in the small storage room," says Steinn. "No need to leave it lying around for all to see. I won't get it done in one evening."

The painting is lying on a high workbench in the side room like a corpse ready for an autopsy. Next to it is a sharp, delicate knife. Hanna looks at the birch grove with her heart in her mouth, momentarily terrified at what they are about to do. The thought of ruining a genuine painting by Gudrun Johannsdottir won't leave her despite all the evidence to the contrary. She still can't get the list from Gudrun's auction in Copenhagen out of her mind and the size of the painting that fits so perfectly.

Steinn sees her doubts, and, as if to draw her into the process, silently hands her the gloves even though she doesn't need to do anything other than watch. Steinn has an expression of utmost concentration on his face, and it looks like he's going to start without further delay.

"Steinn?" asks Hanna.

"Yes," he replies. "Is everything OK?" he adds tersely. "Hadn't we agreed on this?" He doesn't sound annoyed, but his neck has stiffened.

Hanna looks at the painting.

"You haven't told me what came of the tests. Are you sure you can remove the upper layer from the painting? And are you going to do it with a knife?" She can't help raising her voice. "It's just all happening too quickly for me," she says.

She looks at the painting.

"And I think it's a good piece of work. Are we entirely sure? And what about Kristin?"

Steinn shakes his head. "She won't do anything to us. When this is over she'll see that we did the right thing. Just give her a bit of time. Of course, I'll tell you what came out of the tests. And what the knife is for. Just take it easy."

They are standing side by side at the workbench; Steinn pulls the Anglepoise lamp across the bench, flicks the switch, and angles the magnifying glass over the painting. Under the lens the brushstrokes of the sky look like an irregular abstract pattern, and Hanna can clearly make out the lines under the top layer that don't belong to the sky or the clouds but hopefully to the painting *Composition in Blue*.

"The tests showed up various things," begins Steinn. "What I had analyzed were mainly the binding agents in the colors. I had an FTIR analysis done—do you want me to explain what that is?"

Hanna shrugs lightly. This isn't her specialist area.

"Just tell me what came out of it."

Steinn carries on, "This enables you to check whether there are alkyds in the colors. And the samples from both paintings showed up alkyds. That means they must have been painted sometime after 1968 when Winsor and Newton began producing artists' paints with alkyd resin. It wasn't used before then."

Hanna stares at him.

"Is it really that simple? Just like that and we can be sure that the samples are no older than that?"

Steinn nods. "Whoever forged this is a good painter. I didn't exactly have twenty-twenty vision when *Composition in Blue* came to us, and that's why I didn't check it thoroughly enough, but this is well done."

Hanna agrees with this and thinks about his sight. To say he didn't have twenty-twenty vision is putting it mildly.

"It's an exquisite forgery," she says, smoothing over his oversight. "I can't believe it was done in this country. By an Icelandic painter," she adds.

"But it could well be," says Steinn. "Someone living in Denmark, perhaps, who is a specialist on Icelandic painters from this period—who knows? Maybe this is just the start of a new wave of forgeries. In that other forgery case it emerged that novice forgers were doing it. You remember the picture I showed you, where the lower half had been cut off?"

Hanna remembers it. Steinn is right. If someone was going to work as an art forger in Iceland now he would have to become good at his profession.

"It turned out that the top layer of *Composition in Blue* is a yellow finish," says Steinn. "I'll look at it more closely later, but if the painting is new and the top layer is removed then we'll see it and we can examine the colors. There's another sort of finish on this painting, probably this new mock spirit and linseed oil varnish I was telling you about the other day."

Steinn has the knife poised, but then someone comes down the stairs. They shrink back, but it's only the janitor who has been working overtime. He calls good-bye, goes back out, and closes the door.

Putting his gloves back on, Steinn settles himself on a tall stool at the bench with the knife poised. While he examines the surface carefully to decide where best to start, he carries on telling Hanna what came out of the sample analysis. Hanna raises no objections; she trusts he knows what he is doing.

"The sample we took was a cross section," he says. "Right down to the canvas. The base layer is the wash, which is put directly onto the canvas."

He talks calmly and deliberately; this is his specialty.

"On top of that are oil paints, which are free of alkyds. The old colors, that is. That's the painting we think is *Composition in Blue*. On top of this is another wash. Naturally, whoever painted *The Birches* put a wash over the previous painting, and, luckily for us, he has used a poor-quality wash that hasn't adhered well to the oil painting below. The chemical combination is such that I should be able to tease off this second wash easily enough if I go about it carefully. We're lucky that whoever did this was stone broke and couldn't afford decent materials. And, just as I thought, *The Birches* is a mixture of new and old colors."

At last Steinn finds a promising spot up in the right-hand corner of the sky; he inserts the knife very carefully into a bank of white clouds. A minute flake comes loose; they hold their breath. Hanna takes a step back so as not to disturb him, and then moves forward again because she has to watch.

"There's a magnifying glass on the table in the other room," says Steinn, and she goes to fetch it and uses it to watch while he teases off the next sliver with the knife. She hardly dares breathe for fear of distracting him, but Steinn's hands aren't shaking in the least and he works slowly and smoothly. He looks up after a short while. They both look at the section that has been removed. It doesn't answer their question either way.

"What shall we do if this is a completely different painting? By some John Doe?" asks Hanna without expecting a response, nor does Steinn give one.

Then she asks, "Where did Sigfus generally sign his paintings? It would be a stroke of luck to find his signature."

"That's just the problem," replies Steinn. "He rarely did it in the same place. If only we could've been sure it was the bottom right corner, but that's by no means the case. It could just as easily be the left-hand side. Top or bottom, either way. Or not at all. I've looked at everything I can lay my hands on and there's no pattern with him. And I can't see anything on the X-ray."

Steinn remains unperturbed; he just carries on calmly picking tiny specks off the surface of *The Birches*. The picture is already so damaged that repairing it is out of the question. He still hasn't penetrated the wash that lies underneath. Hanna sees that he is hot; he isn't as calm as he appears. He works in silence for a good while; the only sound is a low hum from the air-conditioning and the overhead lights. Finally a small white fleck comes loose and underneath is a glimmer of blue.

On the table next to them is a photocopy from the book about the CoBrA painters that shows a picture of Sigfus and his colleagues, and in the background is a painting that looks like *Composition in Blue*. It's in black-and-white, but the outlines and shapes are unmistakable. On the painting the gallery owns, oblique yellow and white lines run from the right corner where Steinn is scraping off the paint. In the black-and-white photograph they look pale and it's impossible to say what the color is. If it's the genuine painting underneath then Steinn should be able to find a light-colored line roughly where he is working, but the section he has opened up so far is only two to three millimeters.

Hanna stands perfectly still by the table, breathing calmly. Motionless, she follows the delicate movements of Steinn's hands, the tip of his knife, and how he carefully probes for the next speck. He probes a number of times before he teases off a tiny fleck of paint and then another and another. Hanna wouldn't have missed this no matter what the consequences. Relief floods her heart and mind with every millimeter widening the expanse of blue. She feels her belief in what they are doing grow within her; bit by bit she becomes certain that this is right and they have found their treasure. Now is not the time to celebrate, and she doesn't say anything, but she's aware of a tiny invisible smile beginning to break out. Steinn is in a world of his own, but it feels to Hanna like they are breathing in unison. Eventually he looks up and breaks the silence.

"Look at this!"

She leans forward; together they lean forward over the painting and peer at a small patch of blue. Showing in one corner is a fine line of yellow.

Hanna gives a gasp then immediately regains her composure. They both appear calm, but she sees Steinn's hand is quivering. She is longing to jump up and down and shout for joy, fling her arms around him, and tell everyone about it. But she does nothing. She keeps her cool; she senses her foil at the ready and the strength within her. Yes, they probably are right, but now they have to work out their next move.

14

AN UNEXPECTED MOUNTAIN VIEW, SPRING 2005

Hrafn gets a speedy response from Masha. She praises the painting he sent a picture of a few days ago, saying it's glorious. And she wants to do him a favor—to have the painting seen by experts to decide whether it really is by Gudrun Johannsdottir.

Larisa tells me that if the painting does turn out to be by Gurdin then you could get a good price for it. I enjoy this sort of business. Paintings are my hobby, you could even say they are my passion, Masha writes in her e-mail. She misspells Gudrun's name, but Hrafn knows who she means.

His thoughts turn to her private collection in Moscow. Yes, you could certainly say that paintings are her passion. He replies immediately, saying he would be delighted if she would be willing to get the painting assessed and asks her where he should mail it. Masha promptly responds that she will have the painting collected at once. Hrafn is staying in London during this exchange of e-mails, and the painting is in his hotel room in Copenhagen. He has a permanent room in the same hotel where his friend is now installing a sushi bar in the dining room. He gets in touch with the hotel, has the painting brought down to reception, and doesn't give it a second thought; he has other irons in the fire.

Buying and selling paintings is a hobby for him, not his profession, and Hrafn's mind is on his work. He has never been particularly interested in Gudrun Johannsdottir's paintings; her landscapes are too unassuming for his taste, and he hasn't bought any of the abstract paintings she painted later in her career and is best known for. He's not short of money, and it's not the potential for profit that matters here.

Hrafn is curious about Masha. What does this wealthy woman want from him? She hasn't made a move on him; she was evidently going to use Larisa for that purpose, although she has probably now realized that didn't work. All he can assume is that she wants to develop contacts with Icelandic entrepreneurs, some of whom have a reputation for being prepared to take risks and think big. Compared to Mariya Kovaleva, Hrafn and his colleagues are small-fry. Hrafn isn't even among the richest men in the country; he is just one of many who are into big business. But small-fries have their role to play. Small-fries can even transform into fast-moving sharks, if they make the right moves. It's impossible to guess what Masha has in mind.

Hrafn would very much like to forge links with Masha; her hotel chain alone could increase his fish sales twentyfold. His export business has remained static for some time. It's going well enough, but the time for change has come. By partnering with Masha those changes could come sooner rather than later.

When Hrafn arrives in Copenhagen not long after his e-mail exchange with Masha, he finds the painting in his room, wrapped in the same brown paper as before. He is surprised and blames the Russian approach to efficiency. Maybe Masha is all talk and no substance? It doesn't look as if the painting has gone further than to reception and back up again.

His phone rings. It's Vasya. His father's old business colleague.

"I've got some bad news," he says and goes on to tell Hrafn about his wife's death. Vasya's voice is old and weary; he sounds hoarse. Hrafn sympathizes with him, but there's nothing he can do. The funeral has already taken place.

Hrafn is dismayed when he switches off the phone. Vasya and his wife often came to Iceland when he was a boy. He has good memories of them and his father, who showed his best side with them. Now that era is gone forever. He doesn't get time to digest the news because just then his phone rings again. Seeing a Russian number on the screen, he assumes it's Vasya again, but it's Masha's voice on the other end.

"How do you like it?" she asks in her strongly accented English. Hrafn is taken aback. Is she tailing his every move? He only got to the room a few minutes ago.

"I'm not sure what you mean," he replies politely, still thinking of Vasya and his loss. "I've only just got in."

"The painting, of course. How do you like it?" Masha repeats impatiently, her tone excited as a child's. Hrafn looks more closely at the packaging around the painting, which is leaning up against a wall. He was wrong; it has been unpacked and rewrapped. He assumed the painting would be sent to Moscow to be looked at, but obviously that's not necessary. Masha undoubtedly knows competent specialists in Copenhagen.

But he still doesn't understand the question. He knows the painting; he doesn't need to look at it again. She knows he likes it; otherwise he wouldn't have bought it. He looks at the packaging.

"I'm happy with the painting," he says, being careful she doesn't hear the surprise in his voice. "Did you find anything about its history?"

Masha laughs but doesn't answer.

"I knew you'd like it. It's a masterpiece. Now there's no doubt that she, whatever her name is, *dottir*-something, has painted it. Larisa says you could sell it for a good price."

Hrafn assumes that Masha has got a hold of some information that irrefutably links the painting with Gudrun.

"That's good to know," he says. "We should meet up again soon. Are you in Copenhagen?"

But Masha is at home in Moscow. However, before she hangs up she promises to get in touch next time she's in Copenhagen.

Hrafn turns his phone off. Staring at the brown wrapping paper for a moment, he tries to picture the painting in his mind's eye but can't quite recall it in detail. Eventually he picks the painting up, lays it on the bed, undoes the packaging, and looks at a totally transformed painting.

The birch copse has been altered, but what most astonishes Hrafn is the mountain that now rises up from the trees. There was no mountain when he bought the painting. He sits down on the bed, perplexed. He examines the painting more carefully; it doesn't look newly painted, far from it. The paint looks normal.

The wood seems richer than before, the birch trees possess more life, the colors are deeper, and the painting is undoubtedly greatly improved and very like paintings he has seen by Gudrun Johannsdottir. He looks again—no, no signature. He wonders whether Masha has had the painting renovated and this painting was hidden underneath. But that can't be right because in some respects the painting is exactly the same as before; most of the treetops are as they were. The sky doesn't appear to have changed. Then it occurs to Hrafn that his memory is playing tricks on him. The painting has always been like this. But he knows that's not true. He wouldn't have overlooked a whole mountain.

He checks the back of the frame, examines the painting in detail. There's no doubt about it. Masha has got an outstanding forger to alter the painting. To place the scene in the Icelandic countryside and imitate the style of Gudrun Johannsdottir down to the brushstrokes. And he has expressed his delight over it.

Hrafn is not pleased, and for a second he considers destroying the painting. Tear it into shreds and let it disappear. But Masha would not be pleased. Again, he wonders how she knew exactly when he would be returning to his room; she'd called only a couple of minutes later.

What would the market value be of a newly found, prewar painting by Gudrun Johannsdottir? Hrafn calls the gallery in Reykjavik to get some information. The value is good. Would get him a very nice Jeep. He's been thinking about changing. He looks at the painting again, at the back of the frame, no signature, nothing about the origins of the work. The frame hasn't been changed; the painting looks completely authentic. He looks at the picture. He likes it a lot. It's an impressive piece. After a moment's hesitation, he calls his friend, Thor, the lawyer who specializes in copyright. A fellow student from high school days, a fishing buddy and a gym buddy when they're both in Reykjavik. Thor doesn't pick up right away, but Hrafn lets it ring. Thor is often out fishing in the summer, but Hrafn knows that he never goes out without his phone and Bluetooth.

"Well, hello there," says Thor.

"Where are you?" asks Hrafn. "Have you caught anything?"

"I just let one go," replies Thor. "I'm in the Nordura River. Lovely day up here."

Hrafn tells him briefly about the painting. Thor listens carefully, and by the time he replies he's standing on the bank of the river.

"So this Russian woman is in contact with forgers who've done this for her?"

Hrafn concurs and describes Masha's private collection to Thor.

"Do you think the paintings have been forged?" asks Thor, and Hrafn thinks of the rows of paintings on Masha's walls in Moscow.

"No," he replies. "But possibly some of them." He remembers the smell. When they went in he caught a whiff of turpentine and oils. Maybe some of the paintings were brand-new, barely dry.

"I know that Gudrun Johannsdottir sold some paintings at an auction in Copenhagen around 1940," says Thor. "If one of those matched this painting then we'd be sitting pretty. I'll look into it for you when I'm back in town. Talk to my friend Baldur."

Hrafn agrees; he knows what Thor has in mind.

Hrafn is no art forger. He has not made a habit of selling forged pieces. But he has followed the market for a good number of years. He knows that a certain percentage of the art-works in circulation are forgeries; with Thor's help he has man-aged to get rid of a few paintings that he suspected could have been forged, to clean up his collection.

Gudrun Johannsdottir is dead. In his view there's nothing unduly criminal in profiting from a forgery attributed to her, a work that isn't even signed. If he did sell the painting, it would be on the basis that in all probability the painting was by her. And if Thor managed to arrange it that a painting in the auc-tioneer's list in Copenhagen from the time when the original painting was done was listed as exactly the same size as this painting, so much the better. Thor has good contacts and knows someone who is skilled at changing the odd number in an old record in such a way that no one will notice. In this way a paint-ing that originally was sixty-by-eighty centimeters could easily become fifty-by-seventy, for example. Thor has easy access to the records of the gallery in Reykjavik; he simply has to borrow Baldur's keys, no questions asked.

Thor and Hrafn regularly give each other a helping hand. They are businessmen in their different ways. These business dealings are a gray area. Strictly speaking they are illegal of course. Unethical. And yet no one loses by them. Everyone gains. Hrafn, Thor, the auction house. In Hrafn's eyes, such business dealings are all right from time to time but he wouldn't engage in them on a regular basis. And whoever ends up buy-ing this painting will undoubtedly be delighted with this hand-some work of art.

Hrafn hangs up and looks again at the painting; it's unde-niably beautiful and would be a credit to any living room. Give it some time, maybe two or three months, and he will put it back up for auction. In the autumn. As a painting by Gudrun Johannsdottir. The gallery's database will then have documented a painting of this size from the auction list of around 1940.

Hrafn's thoughts then turn to the auction house where he bought the painting. They have a picture of the painting before it was altered. He wants to see it again, to make sure that no one can connect this new painting with the one he bought. People have been caught out by this kind of slipup. Hrafn hurriedly finds the auction house's website, but it's only possible to see sold items from the previous week. He calls them up and gets a picture of the painting he bought e-mailed to him. It is exactly the same as the painting lying on his bed.

Hrafn is relieved but also concerned. It would seem Masha is very well connected, even in Danish auctioneer circles. She has clearly had the image in the database switched and replaced with a picture of the painting as it is now. Obviously it's no problem to find an employee who is willing to get involved in this sort of thing. Invite him to parties on an expensive yacht, to a luxury hotel on a private island, or offer him cocaine and a more beautiful woman than he could dream of legitimately having. Hrafn thinks about Larisa, her gentle movements, the sparkle in her eyes.

It occurs to him that he has met his match in Masha. He has already accepted the painting. Thanked her for it. Expressed his delight. Without opening it. He is angry at himself. This would never have happened to him in another business deal. But how could he have foreseen it? And what would he have said if he had looked at the painting while they were talking? Probably the same. Now he owes Masha a favor and he doesn't know what this favor will entail, only that he can't say no to her.

15

OPENINGS
REYKJAVIK, CURRENT DAY

A shepherd stands under a tree with his crook and his knapsack, leaning up against the broad trunk, watching his flock graze on a broad plain. The morning light falls on a small pond—or is the day drawing to a close? In the distance a village nestles among leafy trees, smoke winds up from the chimneys, bluish like the mountains in the background that soar above the plain, and the clouds are tinged with pink. There is an air of tranquility about the shepherd and his flock; the only thing that brings to mind the transient nature of life is the tree under which he is standing, dominating the center of the canvas. Its crown is dark and leafless, the bare branches standing out against the sky as if in anguish. Man's insignificance in the face of Nature and the Almighty is revealed through the shepherd.

Der einsame Baum, *The Solitary Tree*, is the name Caspar David Friedrich, the nineteenth-century German painter, gave to his work, which is owned by the Alte Nationalgalerie in Berlin and has now come to Reykjavik for the Arts Festival.

It isn't a large painting, only fifty-five by seventy-one centimeters, and it looks lonely there on the second floor gracing the end wall of the exhibition room. Visitors have to peer at the picture to see the shepherd and the sheep or the smoke rising so calmly over the village. The painting has been roped off so they can't get too close to it. Strict security was one of the conditions attached to the loan of this work. The gallery hardly meets such conditions, and if it wasn't for the fact that Herbert Grunewald, patron and cocurator of the exhibition *Landscapes: Past and Present* is the ex-director of the Alte Nationalgalerie, the painting would never have entered the country. Let alone after only a few months to prepare for it.

Much has been made of the painting's debut in the country, and it's not surprising that Baldur and Kristin are rather tense seeing the crowd building up and filling the square outside the gallery. The attendance is even better than they expected. The street artists from Paris who are performing on the square are a big draw. It's the third Saturday in May; the sun is shining and the air is still. It's not only as if spring has arrived, but also summer, on the same day.

Hanna watches the gathering crowd with a slight feeling of surprise. The city has sprung to life today. Families with children and strollers fill the square to watch the artists juggling, fire-eating, and riding on unicycles just like abroad. The cafes on the square have set out tables and chairs and are doing brisk trade—people are drinking beer in the middle of the day as they do in Paris, Copenhagen, or Amsterdam. The square Hanna ran across in the rain and the storm on her way to the gallery on her first day is unrecognizable.

After the incident the week before, Haraldur and Leifur have managed to keep the peace by ignoring each other. Hanna helped Haraldur get his pictures up in the Annexe. She made a point of singing their praises, and while they were hanging them she made out she didn't notice Leifur's installation ranged across the room. Haraldur and Hanna were both pleased with the result.

Haraldur's paintings show no traces of sentimentality, but they possess a poetic quality that appeals to Hanna. His paintings and Leifur's sculpture installation are polar opposites, which is what the exhibition is all about. At first sight Leifur's installation appeared too obtrusive in the room, but he has a keen sense of the overall balance required in the exhibition and was careful not to take over the space. Like most artists of his generation, collaborative working is uppermost in his mind. Moreover, the colors blend with Haraldur's paintings. The rusty-red and iron-gray tones, colorful household paint on the roofing sheets, and discarded wood all reflecting in the panes of glass don't go at all badly with the grassy slopes of Haraldur's paintings.

Jon is showing black-and-white photos of Dutch landscapes, and Anselma has produced an audio piece that can be heard outside the building. The day before, Leifur had told Hanna that he intended to have a display at the opening, but he was reluctant to say what he was going to do. Hanna was doubtful; she would rather he didn't do anything she didn't know about. On the other hand, she didn't want to censor his art. Having made him formally promise that his performance wouldn't harm anyone or any work of art or the building, she gave him her consent, with reservations.

"After the formal opening," was all Leifur said when she asked him when he intended to put on this spectacle. "Won't there be a speech and all that nonsense?"

He smiled slightly as he said this, and Hanna knew he was winding her up. Playing the rebel. She smiled back. Yes, there would be a speech.

Now she can only cross her fingers and trust him. She is waiting for the clock to turn four and is doing one final round of the Annexe when Steinn comes up to her.

"We're about to open." She looks him straight in the eye; he shows no sign of stress. Hanna doesn't understand how he can be so calm. She looks at her folder for the hundredth time; yes, it's all there. She is ready, and, glancing over at Haraldur's paintings as if to draw courage from them, she mentally straps on her mask and primes her foil.

They go into the gallery together, where Kristin and the others are frantically making last-minute preparations for the opening. Edda rushes around with a mop, wiping the floor dry where a minute ago a trayful of sparkling wine went flying over the tiles. She dries it thoroughly because the tiles can be slippery when they're wet. Finally she gives the thumbs-up and the doors are opened. People stream in, hundreds of them filling the airy entrance hall and lower level, but the stairs to the second floor and the painting *The Solitary Tree* is roped off. Everyone who is anyone in cultural and artistic circles in Iceland is there; politicians, bankers, and entrepreneurs all raise their glasses to cultural endeavor.

Hrafn Arnason is chatting to a business colleague when Thor suddenly appears and greets him cheerily. Hanna walks past them, and Thor catches her arm.

"Hanna! I'd like to introduce you to Hrafn here. Hrafn, this is Hanna Jonsdottir," says Thor. "She is director of the Annexe. Hanna, this is Hrafn Arnason."

Hrafn looks at Hanna. They haven't met since they were introduced at the exhibition in Copenhagen. Hrafn doesn't forget a face and immediately remembers her. The mousy one who's an expert in Gudrun Johannsdottir.

Hanna holds out her hand.

"Well, hello, nice to see you again." She is going to say something further, but Hrafn shakes his head imperceptibly. Hanna nods; she understands that he wants to keep the announcement under wraps.

Kristin has already told Hanna about Hrafn. For years she has regularly asked him for money because she knows he collects paintings. An art lover is bound to support the gallery. She finally got an answer out of him, but not the one she expected. In fact, it took her totally by surprise, but now is the moment. Hrafn is going to give the gallery a significant gift, and Kristin is going to announce it publicly at the opening. Hanna immediately realizes that he doesn't want to talk about it in advance.

"Excuse me," she says and continues to thread her way through the crowd.

Hrafn falls silent when she's gone; he is clearly nervous, and Thor tries to change the subject. Hrafn nods absentmindedly. Up to now he hasn't made his hobby public knowledge, and what Kristin is about to say will come as a surprise to many.

Kristin is standing at the mic, which has been set up on the stairs leading to the second floor. To make herself more visible she steps up onto the bottom stair and delivers a short speech.

Hrafn pushes his way through the crowd toward Kristin and stands near the front where he can be seen. He looks somewhat agitated and slides his hands up into his sleeves. At the end of the speech he modestly acknowledges Kristin's thanks with a nod for the magnificent gift that he has donated to the gallery.

Hrafn has decided to stop collecting paintings. The collection he already owns is a reasonable size and is stored in his basement, and the paintings have maintained their value. Of course, he's fortunate the paintings haven't dropped in value, but they haven't increased much either, not compared to the shares in some of the companies he has invested, which have a habit of shooting up overnight. Compared with the stock market there's not much excitement in the art market, and having seen Mariya Kovaleva's collection in Moscow his interest diminished still further. Hrafn realized he was just a small-time collector; he owned nothing really significant by international standards. No Shishkin valued at tens of millions. No Picasso, Matisse, or Rothko. He owned works by Jon Stefansson, Asgrimur Jonsson, and Kjarval. Of the contemporary painters he only has three works by Eggert Petursson.

He decided to let his collection go. Keep the Kjarvals and Eggerts but other than that to turn to his other interest, his horses. Initially, he was going to put all the paintings up for auction, but then he changed his mind. Instead of giving the gallery the funding that Kristin, the director, had harped on him about for a number of years and would enable the gallery to drop the entrance fee, he decided to give them his art collection. This way he would kill two birds with one stone. He would free himself of one aspect of his life that was linked to his father—he is still incapable of looking at a painting without imagining his father's comments or picturing him in his mind's eye, puffing on his cigar. And he will be remembered as an aficionado of art and culture.

Kristin mentions that in America extensions to galleries are often named after their patron, and she promises an exhibition of Hrafn's collection toward the autumn. "Who knows, maybe we'll even get a Hrafn's wing here," she says, smiling broadly at this prospect. Hrafn's mouth puckers slightly at the corners, and he downs his glass of water.

When Kristin has finished her speech, Herbert Grunewald takes over and gives a long talk about his passion for the Icelandic landscape in his rather German-accented English. Then Baldur talks about how the exhibition came about and speaks at length about the value and rarity of *The Solitary Tree*; about the generosity and energy of Herbert Grunewald, who managed to bring the work here; and, not least, he thanks the wealthy benefactor who wishes to remain anonymous and who paid a vast insurance premium for the painting.

"Without him, this would not have been possible," says Baldur, pausing to allow a round of applause.

People are beginning to get restless as he draws his speech to a close, and just at the end Baldur reminds the visitors that there is also an exhibition opening here today in the Annexe under the same theme, *Landscapes: Past and Present*, curated by Hanna Jonsdottir. Finally, Kristin ceremoniously opens the stairs to the second floor. The crowd heads straight up with members of the press and photographers in the lead although no shots of the painting are allowed.

Now the opening of the exhibition in the Annexe begins, and even there it is packed with people. Hanna calls for quiet as she begins her own speech. She isn't accustomed to public speaking and keeps it brief; she thanks the artists who are displaying their work and the gallery for its support of the Annexe.

Just as she finishes her speech and there is a round of applause, a crashing sound reverberates around the room, and Hanna gives a start. Everyone looks around uneasily.

Leifur has carried out his display; he has taken a brick and thrown it at the glass pane separating the internal and external halves of his art installation and smashed the pane into pieces, leaving an opening out onto the street. Three police officers are already standing out on the street in front of the glass wall. Steinn appears at the same time, and Hanna turns to him for advice.

"It's time," he says slowly, calmly. Hanna nods. This wasn't how she'd imagined this moment, but she's ready. The pane can wait, and the broken glass is now part of Leifur's artwork, which extends out onto the sidewalk.

Hanna and Steinn have been preparing for the past few weeks. The press are all here and this is the ideal opportunity to draw attention to what has been going on. This is the course they've agreed to take. Neither of them is willing to wait until Kristin gives the green light to go public about the forgeries, nor does she know what they've done. As things stand, neither Steinn nor Hanna expects charges to be brought. The experience of the big forgery case showed that it's not worth it. And who would bring charges? It's better than nothing then to make the matter public.

Agusta is on the landing of the staircase, where Steinn has put up both the paintings. They now hang side by side, similar but not entirely the same.

The forged version of *Composition in Blue*, false from the outset. The painting the bank bought for fifteen million.

And the painting that lay hidden under *The Birches*. The original work by Sigfus Gunnarsson, the painting that the forger had not expected would be found after all these years, *Composition in Blue*.

There is no painting by Gudrun Johannsdottir; that forgery has entirely disappeared from the surface of Sigfus Gunnarsson's painting.

Agusta has strict instructions from Steinn to ensure that neither painting is removed while he is fetching Hanna.

Hanna looks out over a sea of faces; Steinn touches her arm with his hand. She feels a sense of peace and assurance emanating from him.

"I'll send someone to see to the room and take care of the people. We'll leave this be for the moment. We'll sort it out this evening," Steinn says, meaning the broken glass. Steinn looks taller than usual in his white shirt and dark gray suit. Hanna relies on him. She knows it's reciprocated, and together they edge their way slowly through the crowd toward the stairs where the paintings are waiting. A throng is gathering, and people are flocking to the staircase; many have realized that there's something unexpected going on. Hanna and Steinn make their way up to the landing, where Kristin looks agitated and Baldur is trying to calm her down. Hanna takes the plunge.

"In the end there was no alternative," she says calmly and decisively to Kristin. "It'll serve to draw more visitors anyway."

The press have arrived behind Kristin, and they all fall silent. Steinn makes a brief introduction for the television cameras and points to Hanna. She positions herself in front of the two paintings and waits for silence and a mic. When calm has descended, she opens the third exhibition, an unexpected display of two paintings.

"Thank you for your attention," she reads from the sheet she had secreted in her folder like a most treasured possession. She is careful not to look at either Kristin or Baldur; she knows Kristin is furious.

"About a year ago a large gift was donated to the gallery, one of these paintings that you see here behind me. I expect many of you remember the press coverage of this event and how well attended the opening was when the painting was first shown in public. The painting, which was attributed to Sigfus Gunnarsson, came to us from Denmark. The national bank purchased the painting and donated *Composition in Blue* to the gallery and thereby to the whole nation.

"Some months ago the gallery was also given another painting, attributed to the artist Gudrun Johannsdottir, bought for eight million Icelandic kronur at an auction in Copenhagen."

She pulls a photograph out from under the sheet she is reading and holds it up for all to see and the press to photograph. A picture that shows *The Birches*.

"But before this gift could be made public knowledge, it came to light that everything was not as it should be."

Hanna sees the director, Kristin, edge down the steps and disappear into the crowd with Grunewald's head of silver hair following her. Hanna falls silent. Then she feels Steinn's gaze on her; she must keep going.

"Certain things indicated the painting could be a forgery."

The newswoman who is holding the mic is beginning to get restless, but Steinn puts his hand firmly on her shoulder. "You need to hear the whole story," he says quietly. She gives him an irritated look, but Steinn is undeterred; she relaxes and does as she's told.

"We were considerably surprised when our investigations revealed that underneath the painting attributed to Gudrun was a painting that resembled *Composition in Blue*, no less." Hanna points to the forged painting behind her. "We were faced with a choice, and neither option was inviting. We could leave the painting attributed to Gudrun as it stood, just leave it be. That would have troubled no one but our conscience."

She raises her hand to stop the newswoman, who wants to interrupt again.

"We investigated both paintings thoroughly and then came to the conclusion that *The Birches* attributed to Gudrun would have to be removed from the painting that lay underneath, because that was where the original painting by Sigfus was."

Hanna holds up the photo of *The Birches* again. A loud hubbub ensues as the press all shout out their questions and everyone is talking at once, but Hanna turns around and points to *Composition in Blue*, which the National Bank bought for fifteen million.

"This painting is forged."

Through the barrage of questioning Hanna points to the other work of art, which was once *The Birches*, but in fact is the original piece by Sigfus.

"And here we have the original painting," she says. "*Composition in Blue*, by Sigfus Gunnarsson. It would be true to say that the painting has had a rather convoluted journey to get to the gallery, but here it is."

Hanna and Steinn are stuck on the staircase for a while. Neither Baldur nor Kristin is to be seen, and it's not until the press have fired numerous questions that Hanna manages to get down to the ground floor. She tries to get back into the Annexe, but it's too crowded. She bumps into Agusta, who is also trying to make her way through the crowd, and Hanna is taken aback to see that she's looking distraught.

"Agusta?" says Hanna, but Agusta doesn't answer; she just turns her back and tries to move away. Hanna hears her talking on her cell phone in German and hears her mention Kolbeinn. It immediately occurs to her that Agusta is talking to his father. If he is a foreigner, then that would explain his absence. Edging nearer, she stops a little way behind Agusta, who is now standing by a large pillar, talking in rapid undertones. Concealing herself directly behind the pillar, without giving it a second thought, Hanna listens to what she's saying; curiosity has gotten the better of her.

"You have to believe me, I had nothing to do with this," says Agusta, clearly excusing herself. She goes silent for a moment because the person on the other end is evidently lambasting her. "You've no cause to doubt my faithfulness," she says. "I had no part in this. It's nothing about you. I understand it doesn't look good. Yes, I know that." She manages to get a word in here and there, but the other person seems to be sounding off.

Some familiar faces walk past her, and Hanna looks down and pretends she's fixing something on her boot; she bends almost down to the floor, careful to keep close behind Agusta. She is very upset and lowers her voice, but Hanna can still make out what she's saying.

"What about Kolbeinn? Aren't you going to see him? When are you leaving then?"

She falls silent for a moment.

"Herbert?" she says, but there's no one on the line anymore.

In a flash the pieces of the jigsaw fall into place. Without thinking Hanna jerks up and steps out into the crowd in front of Agusta.

"Is Kolbeinn Herbert Grunewald's son?" she asks firmly, in a low voice so that no one around them will hear. Hanna is still on a high after the exchange with the press on the staircase. Drawing herself up to her full height, she looks straight in Agusta's eyes, leaving her no escape route. "Was it you who told Grunewald about my idea for a landscape exhibition?" she carries on, almost in a whisper.

Edda comes up and wants to speak, but Hanna waves her away.

Agusta also looks Hanna straight in the eye as she replies, "It's wonderful for the gallery to have this work by Caspar David Friedrich," she says, ignoring the first question; there's no need to answer it because Hanna has clearly heard enough to put two and two together.

Hanna looks at her silently. It would be easy to launch an attack on Agusta now. She takes a deep breath and releases it slowly. Agusta is only a few years older than Heba. On her own with a child. Hanna has also been on her own with a child whose father was abroad. Herbert Grunewald is not the most desirable father one could think of. Without a doubt he has never acknowledged Kolbeinn. Hanna knows that the boy's surname is Agustasson. Despite this she can't quite control her anger.

"Why didn't you talk to me?" she hisses. "I would have been willing to work with you on this."

Agusta doesn't respond; she doesn't need to because Hanna knows the answer. Agusta is ambitious and she wanted the credit for it. She wanted to show Herbert what she could do. Baldur was the project manager in name only; she did the legwork. Agusta and Herbert have put this exhibition on between them.

Hanna can't bring herself to have more of a go at Agusta. Her position is not an enviable one. And then Herbert has just laid into her because of what Hanna and Steinn did, which she had nothing to do with. Of course he's hopping mad that the gallery he trusted to display such a valuable work as *The Solitary Tree* should also publicly acknowledge a mistake on a par with *Composition in Blue*. The gallery should have realized immediately that the painting was a forgery, not a year later. And now it seems that Herbert is heading back home without seeing Kolbeinn. Hanna feels for Agusta and eventually calms down.

"It's over and done with," she cuts in when she sees Agusta is about to say something. "We'll talk about it later."

She heads for the Annexe, her mind still on Agusta. After all that, it was Agusta who stole her idea for the exhibition— that's finally come to light. Hanna hadn't needed to mistrust Baldur. She can understand Agusta in a way. Herbert is not so old. Around fifty. He's a handsome man with silver hair, a gleam in his eye, and an attractive smile, very self-assured and influential in the art world.

Hanna knew that Agusta and her colleagues had had the use of Herbert's country house three years before, but not that he had been there himself. That would fit with Kolbeinn's age at any rate, she thinks to herself. And East Borgarfjordur is a unique place, extremely beautiful and romantic. Icelandic spring nights are glorious, heady, each breath intoxicating. And youth and power are attractive opposites.

Herbert enjoys great respect in the art world, but he is a family man; he is not going to cause a scandal with an illegitimate child out in Iceland. It can't be easy for Agusta, she thinks. He's way out of her league and she doesn't even realize it yet.

When Hanna finally sees the whole picture, she empathizes with Agusta. She is pleased with the exhibition in the Annexe, which exceeded all her expectations. That is what matters. And now she's going to head over there and meet her artists and talk to them. She's done what she could, and there's nothing to be gained from being angry at Agusta.

She sees Steinn in the Annexe, standing by the broken windowpane and watching the onlookers and the broken glass.

"I took both the paintings into the basement," he says. "People were crowding in far too close, and they were starting to finger the paintings. And I talked to Kristin—she was absolutely livid."

He suddenly gives a smile, a genuine one, and she smiles back. It's hot in the room, and Hanna feels she's blushing. Out on the street she sees Leifur with some other people, among them Anselma. Through the window she can see that he's talking about his installation; he's gesticulating and smiling happily. Inside the room Haraldur is standing by his paintings and a steady stream of people stop to look and have a chat with him.

Hanna feels a sense of satisfaction welling up inside her. Like after a good battle on the piste. All around her she sees the results of her work. There's Haraldur, who is enjoying the victory of a little comeback on the fine art scene despite everything. Jon, who effortlessly treads his successful path. Leifur and Anselma, who are just starting out. Leifur has challenged himself, he has challenged her, the gallery, and the visiting public, but his work is good; she had already seen that before the exhibition opened, before he smashed the windowpane. That display only made his work better. She sees Anselma talking to the people listening to her audio installation; she's talking animatedly, and Hanna can see that she's satisfied as well. And Steinn is standing by her side, his sight restored as if he had been rescued from the realm of the dead, partially thanks to her. Thanks to Laufey.

Agusta will do well, with or without Herbert Grunewald's help. Hanna knows that she can do it without him; at some stage she will realize that for herself.

And then Hanna doesn't think any more about the others for the moment. Not about *The Birches*, which has now disappeared, or about *Composition in Blue*, not about Gudrun Johannsdottir or Sigfus Gunnarsson. Not about Kristin, Baldur, or Herbert Grunewald. Not about Frederico, not even about Heba. Not about children who suffer and end up in trouble, not about Kari or how he'll come through. Not about her friends, or about tomorrow. This is her moment.

16

IN THE ARTIST'S STUDIO, SPRING 2005

The painting on the easel is almost complete. Larisa just has a few minor details to go over; the texture on the half-moon could be a little coarser, but not too much so. Sigfus was a meticulous artist and his abstract paintings are no botch job. She has already gone a number of times to the exhibition in the new Cultural House to study his paintings more closely—she can almost tell what size brush he used from the fine details in the brushstrokes. Larisa is a professional.

It was Hrafn Arnason who unwittingly gave her the idea to move into the Icelandic market. Until that point she and Masha had focused on the Russian market, but it was becoming increasingly dangerous to get valuable pieces into circulation. However, a small market, like the Icelandic one, is undeveloped and buyers are not connoisseurs, so the danger is minimal. This is where Masha comes into it; one word from her about a desirable painting on auction is enough for the investor to buy blind over the phone. Masha knows vast numbers of investors, and Icelanders are no different from others in such matters. Her art collection is incomparable and praised for its rare and valuable works. She shows it now and again and only then for individuals who move in influential circles and can have a word in the right ear.

The two women complement one another and they don't correct the common misconception that Masha is the boss and Larisa is her assistant. In reality it's the other way around. Not even Masha is aware of Larisa's assets or the scale of her business dealings in the art world. Larisa doesn't only handle her own paintings; she is a big-time arts trader, although very few people are aware of these transactions as they are rarely done in her name.

The painting is finished. Larisa takes a few steps back, satisfied with her initial attempt at the style of the Icelandic artist Sigfus Gunnarsson. She took a long time studying the blue color his paintings are famous for. Larisa isn't familiar with this shade of blue; she can't compare it with anything else in the environment around her, neither in the light nor the landscape, but then she's never been to Iceland, where this color blue springs from. On her palette it always became too dull; she had to discipline herself very firmly to allow the cobalt blue to light up the canvas with its clean, clear tone. The same can be said of the color yellow, but in the end the painting worked extremely well. Now it needs time to dry, and Larisa has all the equipment and materials needed to make it age convincingly by about seventy years in a matter of days. Masha will then take care of the auction house, where she has reliable contacts on the staff.

Larisa looks with satisfaction at the results. She appreciates a job well executed. She is a prolific and versatile artist whose work methods are polished and disciplined. Her knowledge is extensive; she was outstanding at school, at university, and then in her job as an art historian. It was in this role back home in Saint Petersburg that she was often asked to examine paintings, to assess their origin and their worth and whether the painting was genuine. More often than not they were forgeries, and this trend was ever increasing, in direct proportion with the nouveau riche in Russia who were intent on buying a part of their national history to hang up on their walls at home. The nineteenth-century romantic painters were always particularly popular, and their paintings, forged or genuine, sold just as fast for huge sums.

In the end Larisa wanted her share as well. She didn't care to live her life on a civil servant's salary, shut in an art gallery, and she began to study the forgers' methods. One of the most popular was to buy a reasonably priced German or Danish painting by a little-known artist from the eighteenth or nineteenth century. A painting of a rural scene that was easy enough to make a bit Russian. Add some hens or a Russian country cottage into the picture, something characteristic of paintings by Russian artists. Who can possibly distinguish a Russian country lane from a German one? And she was very good at it. In just a few years she built up contacts internationally and then moved to London and Copenhagen.

Now standing here, she admires her own skill. The next painting that awaits her is of a different nature, and, unusually, Larisa is not working for money this time. She intends to capture a man who she can't get out of her head. He hasn't let himself be seduced yet, but she knows it's only a matter of time. She has seen the look in his eyes and felt the way he shrinks back, as if from an open fire. Larisa isn't bothered about his wife and children; that sort of life and those who lead it are of no interest to her. Hrafn is different. She's expecting a parcel from him any minute. She's going to give him a painting, but he doesn't know it yet—maybe he'll never know.

When the deliveryman arrives with the painting wrapped in brown paper, everything is ready. Numerous prints of Gudrun Johannsdottir's paintings have been pinned up on a large wall in the northern light; on the slanting roof of the studio is a specially made window that can be covered or opened to let the light in as desired. Larisa opens the parcel and puts the painting up on the easel. A Danish painting of a birch copse on a summer's day, the bright sky in the background, the forest floor vibrant with varying shades. Not a bad painting, but about to take a quantum leap; a mountain is about to rise up from the birch trees, the treetops will bend and become gnarled. Gudrun's passionate rhythmic brushstrokes suit Larisa well. She will carry this off without a hitch, and all the while she's painting she thinks about Hrafn.

17

CHOCOLATE
REYKJAVIK, CURRENT DAY

The first thing Hanna does on Monday after the opening is to go up the staircase. *Composition in Blue* has gone. She goes back down again. Few people have come into work today; the gallery is closed. Hanna's footsteps echo loudly on the tiled floor in the lobby. She meets Steinn in the corridor leading to the open-plan offices. They haven't spoken since the opening. He grips her arm excitedly.

"Thank goodness I saw you! Come with me a moment—I must show you something."

Hanna follows Steinn down into the basement with mixed feelings. He no doubt wants to show her something in connection with the two paintings, something they overlooked. When they get down, she sees the two paintings up against a wall over in the corner, wrapped in polyethylene, but Steinn walks past them and on toward the large shelves at the back of the room. He indicates that she should follow as he leads in that direction.

"I've been meaning to show you this for some time."

Steinn picks two paintings up off the shelf and leans them up against the wall. They are landscape paintings by Gudrun Johannsdottir, but Hanna hasn't seen them before. Steinn points her to the corner of one of the paintings. The signature appears to have been painted over, but the work is signed by Gudrun in the other corner. Hanna looks at Steinn. She can hardly believe her own eyes.

"Are you saying that…?"

Steinn says nothing for the moment; he just looks at the paintings.

"That's what I fear," he says. "These aren't new acquisitions; the gallery's owned them for some years. But look at these." He takes two more paintings down from the shelf, pictures that Hanna knows and was looking at just a few weeks before. She breathes more easily. These are landscape paintings from early on in Gudrun's career. She glances at them briefly.

"Yes, this is entirely different." She looks at the black sheep again. Steinn had deliberately covered them up.

He puts the paintings back on the shelf. "As you can imagine, I have discussed these with Kristin. But you know what she's like."

Hanna looks at him questioningly. "No, I'm not sure I do," she says. "I don't fully understand Kristin."

Steinn shakes his head.

"She's just a snob with no balls. That's all there is to it. Between us we've been arguing about this for a number of years. She always avoids anything that could be damaging to her or the gallery. I wanted to use the opportunity when the big forgery case was going on and go to court about these paintings, but Kristin hemmed and hawed so long that eventually it was too late. But she never said no, not directly, just like this time."

Steinn straightens the paintings on the shelf.

"When we got *Composition in Blue* I was too concerned about my eyesight to be able to investigate it properly. You know what the outcome was there. The director of the National Bank who donated the painting is a friend of Kristin's, as you can imagine."

Hanna looks at him. "I didn't think Kristin was so—unprofessional," she says.

"Kristin's all right really," says Steinn in her defense. "She fights like a lion for the gallery. She's an outstanding fund-raiser, has lots of good contacts, and has a nose for exhibitions that will draw the crowds. And it was Kristin who got the Annexe going," he adds. "But she does like parties, especially when the social elite are all there. She knows that the bank director and Elisabet would both give her the cold shoulder if she went public with this now. And boycott the gallery—the National Bank has given financial support to our exhibitions every year. Maybe she really only intended to bide her time."

"Do you want to bide your time with this?" Hanna asks straight-out, and Steinn doesn't answer.

"I think it would strengthen our case to have two professional opinions," he replies instead. "That of a curator and an art historian. But as things stand, I don't really want this to go beyond the gallery. There's enough of a fuss for now. It would be too damaging for the gallery right now. It would create a mistrust we don't deserve. There's no urgency. These paintings are just sitting here in the basement. We need to let this storm die down first."

Hanna is relieved because she doesn't want another battle just yet. But she recognizes that these paintings are of a different quality than the one they were dealing with in the previous weeks. These are amateurish forgeries and probably wouldn't be hard to verify. Then the gallery could at least make the decision not to display the paintings whether the case went to court or not. They won't go to court over *Composition in Blue* or *The Birches* either; the only thing coming out of that debacle is that the gallery gained an original work of art instead of two forged ones. That's maybe not such a bad outcome.

Hanna and Steinn have gotten the pieces of the puzzle before them, but the picture isn't complete. They don't know who painted the forged *Composition in Blue* from scratch, from Sigfus Gunnarsson's sketches. And still less who painted a Danish birch wood over Sigfus's *Composition in Blue* when Christian Holst, the butcher, owned the painting. Nor who bought *The Birches* from Holst's estate and resold it at auction.

Having put all the paintings back in their place, Steinn looks at Hanna.

"What do you think?" he asks. "Are you up for it?"

Hanna realizes that he wants an ally against Kristin. Steinn can use Hanna for his own ends; she is an outsider, on a temporary contract, and she hasn't worked with Kristin for the five years he has. Hanna doesn't need to give it a second thought before answering yes.

A staff meeting is called just after Hanna and Steinn come back up from the basement. Baldur, Hanna, Steinn, and Agusta are sitting around the meeting table when Kristin arrives. She looks weary and no colorful shawl adorns her shoulders today. Coffee is on the table, and they help themselves in silence.

Baldur pours a cup for Hanna, and she smiles at him. When all's said and done, he has proved himself to be the friend he always claimed to be. Baldur looks at her slightly surprised, and Hanna feels ashamed that she's been so cold toward him for no good reason these past months.

Kristin doesn't refer to the unexpected stir over the weekend; she acts as if nothing had happened. She simply talks about how much interest the painting by Friedrich, *The Solitary Tree*, aroused and how the number of visitors exceeded all expectations. She praises Baldur and Agusta for their hard work in preparing for it, and she praises Hanna for the unusual exhibition in the Annexe; she particularly mentions that a number of people came to her and expressed how pleased they were to see paintings by Haraldur. After the gallery was closed on Saturday, the windowpane that Leifur broke with his spectacle was replaced. Kristin stresses that it must not be broken again while the exhibition is running, and Hanna agrees, but she does not apologize for herself or excuse Leifur. She waits for Kristin to talk about the two paintings, but she doesn't mention them, as if the incident had never happened. Hanna doesn't say anything either; occasionally she glances over to Steinn, who is looking down into his coffee cup and doesn't join in the conversation. Finally Kristin announces the meeting is over. They stand up to leave, and, as Hanna is in the doorway, Kristin beckons her over.

"Hanna dear, wait a moment."

Hanna looks at her in surprise but sits back down at the table while the others leave the room.

Kristin does not talk for long, and Hanna hears her out. She thanks Hanna for her good work. Praises her exhibition again and talks about the positive reaction from the public. She refers to how well the gallery and Annexe have worked together since Hanna came. Thanks her for her work with the outdoor works of art. She says that Steinn was right when he recommended her for the job. She then ends by saying what a great shame it is that she cannot keep Hanna on at the gallery. They need to tighten their belts, and at the end of the month Agusta will take over as director of the Annexe. They will take into consideration Hanna's terms of employment, and she will be given substantial severance pay.

Kristin doesn't give Hanna the chance to reply; she just stands up and holds out her hand, repeating that Agusta will take over at the end of the month, in a week's time, before showing her out as politely as possible given what has just taken place.

Hanna passes Baldur's office on her way down after the conversation with Kristin. He beckons to her, but she pretends not to hear and hurries on down the stairs. She doesn't know if she is relieved or disappointed, but she is definitely angry. Her phone rings on the stairs. It's the town mayor's office.

"The mayor can meet you in fifteen minutes," says the assistant, whom Hanna has spoken to many times before, trying to pin the mayor down for a meeting. She nearly bursts out laughing. Is that how business is done at the council? In fifteen minutes? She hesitates before answering. Should she go, help Agusta out before she takes over? Hanna keeps on walking and asks the woman on the other end to hold the line a moment. Finally she answers.

"I'm sorry," she says. "I can't come right now."

When she gets to her desk Agusta is on the phone, Edda is typing fast with one finger, and Steinn is sitting at the computer.

She will miss him. A week is a very short time. She looks at the calendar. Not even a week, five days.

She won't say anything to her colleagues yet; maybe they already know about it. She never did become part of this little family, and now she never will.

Sitting down at her computer, Hanna casts her eye over her desk. It's neat and tidy; admittedly there are piles of paper on it, but they are all neatly ordered. The website has been regularly updated. The landscape exhibition extends into June, and then there's the summer exhibition in conjunction with the gallery. Hanna has already decided on two exhibitions for the autumn, but Agusta will have to oversee those now. She glances over to Agusta, who is still on the phone.

It'll be good for the Annexe to have close connections with influential people in the art world, she thinks to herself without sarcasm. Agusta will do a good job.

Hanna is absentminded and cannot concentrate. She looks out at the May sun shining on the cold blue sea; there are still patches of snow on Mount Esja. Thoughts whirl through her head.

Kari. She must do something for Kari before she goes.

Heba. How happy she will be to see her mom come home earlier than expected. Hanna longs to see her daughter again.

Work. She will have to find herself a new job. Maybe she could go back to her old place. There's no urgent need to think about that. The severance pay that Kristin offered her belies her comments about the need to tighten their belts.

Last but not least, she thinks about Frederico, and she still doesn't know what she wants. Now she needs to make a decision much sooner than she'd anticipated. Hanna looks over to Steinn. Well, she won't be able to help him as she'd intended.

It was because of Steinn that she was offered this post. Not because of her international experience in the contemporary art scene or her background as a specialist in Gudrun's landscape paintings. After all that she has achieved in her job abroad in Amsterdam in recent years, she finds this rather ironic.

Steinn thought he was losing his sight; he needed someone to assist him in exposing the art forgeries. Hanna is sorry not to be able to carry on helping him, but she knows that he will carry on regardless. Steinn highly recommended you when we were looking for someone, Kristin had said. That's what had tipped the balance. And he is utterly indispensable to the gallery.

It's plain to see, Steinn looks after so many aspects of the running of the gallery and he's been there for a long time. If he left, it would take at least two people to replace him. He will obviously carry on despite the commotion over the weekend. Hanna senses that Kristin has a lot of respect for Steinn. He will find a way to reconcile with her.

Later that day Hanna goes out and buys chocolate cakes for their coffee break. She came with chocolate and she will say her good-byes with chocolate.

18

A CLAUDE GLASS

Hanna wants to see Kari before she leaves. She has found out through Gudny's contacts that the family has been split up. The children have each been placed with a different family. Kari has been relocated to a new foster family after the first one gave up on him because he kept disappearing. Now he is apprenticed to a couple on a farm. When Hanna gets in touch with them and tells the foster mom that she wants to give Kari a present before she leaves, the woman responds warmly, so Hanna decides to rent a car for the day on the last weekend in May. At the last minute she has another idea. She is nervous about going on her own to meet him. Things didn't exactly go well the last time.

On Saturday morning Steinn comes around in his Volvo. He comes up to her flat and waits quietly while Hanna gets ready. This is the first time they have met, or even spoken, outside of work, and the silence between them feels awkward as they both know that it is also the last time they will meet. This awareness casts a shadow over the day that Hanna can't shake off; she avoids looking Steinn straight in the eye, and they are careful not to touch.

This time Steinn is driving; Hanna has a map of the Western District with the name of the farm marked. They drive without stopping on the way. Their conversation is stilted, and Hanna turns on the radio to lighten the atmosphere. She doesn't need to say that she is sorry to be leaving, that they can't continue their investigations together. He knows that.

By midday they've arrived. The farm is in a beautiful setting at the foot of a grassy slope. There are cows and sheep, hens, a dog, and horses for hire. The foster parents are warm and friendly and invite Hanna and Steinn in to join them at the lunch table, where Kari is sitting with the farmer and a laborer. The farmer's wife serves them their food, and Hanna feels she has gone back in time. They talk about what's in the news, but the conversation is mostly about the sheep and lambs; the lambing is just coming to an end. The farmer and the farm laborer exchange brief bits of news about the ewes and their lambs; they were up all night. Kari sits quietly and doesn't join in the conversation.

After lunch Hanna goes out to fetch two books from the car. One is a history of twentieth-century Western art. The other is an introductory book about graffiti artists. Kari takes the books without a word; he doesn't thank Hanna, doesn't look her in the eye. She thinks about his life, his sisters who are now with their different foster families in Reykjavik. She chokes up and wants to say something, but the words won't come. They sit there in an embarrassed silence with the farmer's wife until Steinn eventually comes to the rescue.

"What have you got there, son?" he asks, and Kari proudly shows him an amateurish tattoo on his right arm, which is peeking out from under his sleeve.

"It's my crew," he says, unabashed. "Our tag."

Steinn nods. "Well done. Did you design it?"

Kari nods silently. Silence envelops him, a silence full of stubbornness, anger, and grief.

"Do you sometimes come into town?" Steinn carries on in his calm manner.

Kari shakes his head glumly. Hanna looks across at the farmer's wife sitting next to Kari, who is following the conversation. Hanna wonders whether they are just using him as cheap labor.

"We go from time to time," she says. "It's not so far," she adds, directing her words at Kari. There is fondness in her tone, and Hanna is relieved. So he's not being made to work. She can't see any other children around.

"Drop in and see me," Steinn says to Kari. "You know where to find me."

Kari stares stolidly at the floor.

"I've got an outside wall for you if you want, you and your crew. You can do what you want on it. It's a large wall around the back, and it's a mess right now because the little taggers never leave it alone. You can do what you like."

Kari doesn't say anything, but he shoots Steinn a look and then turns away, apparently disinterested.

They leave shortly afterward. They get into the car in silence; Steinn drives off and the silence hangs in the air for some time.

"He'll come, maybe," says Steinn eventually. "He'll be drawn. He'll look at those books, although he'll do it when no one is around. You'll see," he says to Hanna encouragingly, but she is looking out of the window, trying to hold back the tears forming in the corners of her eyes. She swallows a hard lump in her throat and doesn't say what she's thinking about this broken family whose fate upsets her so.

"Thank you," she says.

Hanna thinks back. To when her father left them, when they suddenly stopped being a family. She surreptitiously dries a tear and, suddenly, without thinking it through or coming to any conscious decision, she cannot wait to be back home.

She feels as if she'd been struck blind, as if she'd not seen what it was that mattered even though she'd been thinking about it all these months. There is no question of breaking up the family. No matter what Frederico has done or may do.

The feeling is so strong and so tangible that she needs to get it out of her system; she cannot go on another second sitting still in the car and so she suggests to Steinn that they stop and get a breath of fresh air. Shortly after Steinn pulls off on a side road. They are in an area of summer cottages with paths through the birch trees, and they set off with nothing further in mind than a short stroll.

Hanna leads the way. The sun comes out from behind the clouds and it's warm and bright. When they reach a bench made from a solid tree trunk beside the path, Hanna takes a seat and closes her eyes against the sun. She's about to leave this country and doesn't know when she'll be back. She feels the sun warming her face. Steinn sits next to her, and, pulling something out of his pocket, he hands it to her. She screws up her eyes against the sun.

"I think this is a good moment." He's handed her a small black box, about the size of her palm.

Hanna looks at him in surprise; it hadn't occurred to her to give Steinn a present.

"Aren't you going to open it?"

She lifts the lid off the box. Inside is a little silver holder, rather like a cigarette case, engraved on the lid. When she opens it she sees a curved, oval mirror. She lifts it out and looks at her reflection, but obviously that is not the idea because she just sees a dark, distorted reflection of herself. Steinn laughs.

"I found this on the auction house's website," he says. "They don't only sell paintings, but all kinds of stuff." Hanna tells him about the Russian dolls and the Chinese tree and how she had wondered what sort of people bought artifacts there.

"So it's people like you."

"I didn't buy it immediately. I'd been aware of it for some time."

Hanna wonders when he'd bought it. Perhaps when Kristin told him Hanna would be laid off? After their meeting with Kristin, when Steinn stayed on? Before? Or later?

That is neither here nor there. Steinn is giving her a unique and beautiful gift, whatever it is.

"I simply had to buy this for you, because it's just what you need."

"What is it exactly?" asks Hanna finally. Steinn takes the mirror, and, lifting it up in front of her face, he shows her how she can capture a mirror image of the landscape behind them. In the mirror it resembles an eighteenth-century painting. Squinting, Hanna smiles.

"Wow! That's marvelous!" She sees the birch trees in the mirror start to look like an old painting.

"It's called a Claude glass," says Steinn. "People used it in the eighteenth and nineteenth centuries to view the landscape. To see the landscape as it looks in Claude's paintings."

Hanna is very familiar with the seventeenth-century landscape artist Claude Lorrain and his paintings. She is still smiling. It's exactly what she needed. She looks at Steinn; now would be the perfect moment to kiss him. She knows he is thinking the same.

1 9

AN ARTIST PAYS HIS RENT
COPENHAGEN, 1943

Sitting erect on the light green corduroy sofa, the lady of the house regards her lodger with a questioning look, while the young man, an artist, stands timidly in the doorway. There is a tray on the ornate coffee table next to the sofa with a cup of tea and candies in a crystal bowl. She proffers the bowl; her hand is lily white, soft, and well manicured.

"May I offer you a sweet? You look so downcast."

The artist enters the room hesitantly, stepping cautiously across the shiny parquet flooring, and is careful not to walk on the woven rug. He reaches out and picks up a sweet with his finger and thumb; he is so hungry that his hand is shaking.

"I hope there isn't a problem with the rent—again?" She looks up sharply and contemplates his old worn jacket and the hole in his shoe. "Why don't you take proper care of your appearance?" She picks up her embroidery, which is lying next to her on the sofa; she is not a woman to sit idle.

Her lodger doesn't reply; there is no point. He cannot pay the rent; he is relying on her mercy, on the goodwill of the butcher's wife, who is totally ignorant of art and doesn't know what it is to be hungry. The paintings on the walls around her are from the red-haired woman's collection, the woman who loves art, Elisabeth Hansen, who needed to sell off her whole collection.

But her paintings are not all here, just those that any visitors are already familiar with. The butcher's wife seeks justification for her bourgeois existence through art. She looks for the familiar; she likes what she knows. The role of art is to reveal the bourgeoisie in the most flattering light, to endorse the accepted values of society. If she cannot see what a painting is saying, then it doesn't appeal to her.

An idea suddenly occurs to him.

"I was wondering whether you might like a beautiful painting of a birch wood. You don't have many paintings here that reveal the Danish countryside at its most beautiful." She looks at him and thinks about it for a moment. He treads carefully, like a cat around a saucer of cream. He wants to delay the rent and paint a picture for her instead. She reaches out for a sweet. Lays her embroidery down in her lap.

"I saw a painting in the attic, which I thought no one would be interested in," he adds. "An abstract painting, blue and yellow. It's just going to rack and ruin up there. I could maybe paint over it."

The lady of the house gazes out of the window; she is beginning to get bored of this conversation, of his timidity, and of the awkwardness of the situation. Why doesn't the man just get himself a job? But then she decides to give him one more chance. She is a good woman. But if he doesn't pay his rent in a fortnight, then he's out. Relative or not, that's the way it is. He hasn't once paid his rent on time this autumn; he's been one week late, three days late, or five days late. This obviously cannot go on; it's just too unreliable. It would be better to have a girl, someone from the college for housewives, and then she could also help out with the domestic chores. But then it might be necessary to put a heater up in the attic room. Then again, spring is just around the corner.

She tries to recall the painting he is referring to. It must have been part of the collection Christian bought from Mrs. Hansen. Blue and yellow…Ah yes, she remembers it now. She couldn't stand the thing. It was awfully ugly and she had asked for it to be taken away.

"You're welcome to paint over it," she says. "It's a worthless piece. An abstract painting! No Dane is interested in that sort of thing. Please do just paint a pretty birch wood over it. There's nothing in the world as delightful as a Danish birch."

She smiles at him and extends the bowl of sweets to him again. What a relief, he thinks. Now he can buy himself a meal this evening. If he also buys some oatmeal, that should last him the week as well. If he goes down to the harbor early enough each day he might also get some work unloading the boats for a few days. There's no other work to be had, no matter how hard he looks. But his joy is short-lived.

"You may have two weeks' grace to pay your rent on this occasion. You've never paid on time since you first started living here. We'll look on the painting as an additional remuneration because we've been so generous, despite these delays, but I'm afraid this can't carry on. I'm giving you notice to quit at the end of this month. You should have the painting finished by then."

She takes a sip of her tea and smiles at him.

"The room is clearly too expensive for you. It's hardly too much to expect you to pay on time, is it? It costs a lot to run this home, you understand. My husband has to look after his affairs."

At which the lady picks up her embroidery again; she rings the bell, and the maid comes running. The lodger passes her in the doorway. When he goes out into the corridor, to the stairs leading up to the unheated attic he has rented these past months, he hears the lady of the house telling the maid to prepare a three-course evening meal. In his head he pictures a birch copse, his assurance of a roof over his head for the coming weeks. What will happen after that, he doesn't know.

ABOUT THE AUTHOR

 Ragna Sigurdardottir is a native of Reykjavik, Iceland, and the author of five novels. She studied French and fine arts in Aix-en-Provence before attending the Icelandic School for Arts and Crafts. After earning a bachelor's degree in fine arts from the Jan van Eyck Academy in the Netherlands, she worked as an artist and writer in Rotterdam and later in Denmark. She eventually returned home to Iceland, where she spent a decade working as an art critic for Icelandic newspapers. Currently she studies art theory at the University of Iceland and is writing her sixth novel. She lives with her husband and their two daughters on the outskirts of Reykjavik, just down the street from the North Atlantic Ocean.

ABOUT THE TRANSLATOR

 Born in 1957, Sarah Bowen graduated from University College London with first class honors in Icelandic Studies. Her translations include "My Kingdom and Its Horses," a short story by Audur Jonsdottir and *The Creator*, a novel by Gudrun Eva Minervudottir. She and her husband are based in Surrey, England, where she also works as a freelance BSL interpreter. They have three grown-up daughters.